Gillian ('Gill') Mather ha ... es
and at various times ha ... as
covered by general p ... y,
employment, civil litigat ... ill
ran a small solicitor's p ... ter
until 2020. She is a mem ... sex
and Suffolk, including Write Now. ... ere
previously published under the pen name of Julie Langham.

Gill has published eight full-length novels on Kindle, the first five being a series of romantic-cum-crime novels set in Colchester around a fictional law firm and featuring the same main characters over a number of years. The last book in the series is also a paranormal romance. Some are available as paperbacks.

As The Clock Struck Ten, a crime/mystery/psychological drama about an accusation of sexual abuse, is the sixth novel. *The Unreliable Placebo,* a rom-com with a difference, is the seventh novel. And the eighth novel, *Class of '97,* is a mystery/psychological drama.

There are six novellas so far in the Roz Benedict Detective Novellas series, of which *Compromised* is the first. Further novellas in the series are planned.

Gillian Mather April 2022

Also by Gill Mather

(In a the same series as *Compromised*)
Cut Off
Conflicts of Little Avail
Conjecture Most Macabre
Le Frottage
Confounded

(Colchester Law World series)
The Ardent Intern
Threshold
Relatively Innocent
Reasonable Doubts
Beyond The Realms

As The Clock Struck Ten
The Unreliable Placebo
Class of '97

COMPROMISED

GILL MATHER

This paperback edition published in 2022 by Inquisitor Books,
an imprint of Write Now! Publications

A CIP catalogue record for this book is available from the British Library

Paperback ISBN: 978-1-912955-27-5
ebook ISBN: 978-1-912955-19-0

To Write Now! They're always there

.

PART I

Prologue

Hatford, Hertfordshire – June 2015

THE second floor attic studio flat was small and cramped, the terraced house in which it was situated being unsuitable for conversion into two flats, let alone three, but developers always squeezed the extra few thousand pounds of profit out of any building project.

Romanian twenty-something, Ileana Bratianu, nowhere to go this Friday evening, was on the verge of getting ready for bed early to watch the TV in comfort. She was about to start undressing when a thud and the noise of breaking glass made her freeze. It sounded as though it was in the building, right outside her door in fact.

"Dumnezeule!" My goodness!

Her door shook. Incredibly, someone was trying to break the door down. There was no other way out, no fire escape, no flat roof or balcony onto which to escape and possibly climb to the ground. There was no one she could call to for help. To her certain knowledge, the residents of the two flats below would be out working nights usually or, if not, socialising. But she called:

"Ajută-mă. Ajutor." Help me. Help

The flimsy door gave way. Ileana looked frantically around for her mobile phone, but it was in her bag which was hanging on the back of the door and, at this moment, the door was swinging on its hinges, banging against the wall. Terrified, she backed away, watching the intruder gain entry.

"Ce? … De ce? … Nu!" What the…? Why? No!

She gave a hopeless cry.

"Matei. Matei."

The intruder's form cast a lengthening shadow across Ileana, produced by the overhead light, as the person walked slowly towards her.

Chapter 1

THE night was dark and turning a little chilly. The canal path was bordered by converted Victorian industrial buildings containing, as well as the bars and shops at ground level, loft-style, balconied apartments above. A swish, new modern apartment appealed to Mal but they were expensive both to buy and to own. Therefore he'd bought a terraced house instead a few streets away, only a short walk from the canal path.

And not far to stagger back either after a night on the lash, including the detour via and several hours spent at the nightclub. A girl of interest to the constabulary lived in one of the terraced houses on his route home.

He looked up towards the second floor skylight windows of the studio flat in the roof space in which he knew the girl lived. The lights were on, which was unusual at this time.

The girl had reported multiple threats against her; threats made by phone and text to her mobile, by email, by post even. She told police that items had been put through the letterbox addressed to her. For example, squashed, dead birds in padded envelopes with messages telling her that she'd be next. These and the rest had been examined but they led nowhere and the police had begun to speculate that she'd created the messages herself to get attention.

Not much was known about the girl. She had told them barely anything about herself. She didn't appear to trust anyone. And with no extraneous information, no co-operation from the girl herself, the investigation stalled.

But Mal always looked up at her windows when walking past and usually there were no lights on late into the night. Once, a few weeks ago, he had pressed the buzzer on seeing lights in the window but there'd been no answer. He'd reported it at the station the following day and someone had phoned the girl at work and it turned out she was OK.

Tonight, though, he went round the back of the row of buildings. There was what was referred to as a 'back passage' cutting through between the rears of two rows of houses. His own house backed onto such a passage with a mirroring terrace the other side. When he'd read this phrase, 'back passage', in his solicitors' contract report relating to his own purchase, rambling on about a right of way, he'd laughed out loud and had nearly emailed back a lewd comment.

Having pushed open the back gate and having seen that the back door of the building was open, Mal went in and walked along the narrow corridor towards the front of the house where the stairs were located. He was glad that he'd opted for a self-contained terraced house where no one else could leave the doors open or access the building without some effort. Probably a tenant had thoughtlessly failed to close the back door.

Nevertheless, it was a little worrying. He should investigate, he told himself. He'd rather go home, but just in case, as the door had been open anyway, he'd better go up and see if anything was wrong. Still, he paused for a short time, collecting himself. He tried the light switch but nothing happened and the stairs before him were pitch black.

MAL walked nervously up the stairs. He pulled out his smart phone and switched it on, angling it this and that way so that light fell on the treads and walls. He climbed slowly. At one point, he crunched something underfoot.

"Shit!"

He peered around him. There was no sound in the building and nothing coming from outside either. The ground and first floor flats were probably empty at this time, both lots of occupiers having evening jobs. At the top of the second flight, light spilled from the open door of the second floor flat.

He stood on the small landing, frowning. The door looked as though it'd been damaged. Quite possibly a burglar, or an assailant or other intruder, might still be in there. They might be armed. He mentally squared his shoulders. He'd no alternative. He pushed the door further open and tiptoed in.

The open plan bedsit was in turmoil. All was quiet and Mal cautiously searched it. The girl wasn't in the main small open sitting area. She wasn't in the bed and the bed was still made. She wasn't in the minuscule kitchen either which was open to the main living area.

He entered the bathroom and involuntarily sniffed the air. It smelled of excrement and pee. The shower curtain was drawn across the bath. In films and dramas, there was always a dead body when you pulled back the shower curtain.

Mal drew the curtain. He looked for a second at Ileana Bratianu. Fair-haired, she was lying in the bath fully clothed, bulging blue eyes wide open in death. He held his left hand up to his face, cupping his nose against the smell, and he quickly looked away.

Chapter 2

MUFFLED, unclear conversation and noise from along the corridor reached the DI's room in which Mal had been waiting for some time. He should've gone straight home after a boozy Friday night out with his mates at a bar and then a club. He should never have gone up to the girl's flat.

It was the first warm night this year and they'd been able to exit the crush inside the pub and collar one of the few free tables overlooking the canal. It should've been a bloody good evening, but instead–

Suddenly the door opened wider.

"Right. You're off the investigation," said the DI, coming in and sitting down.

Mal groaned and put his head in his hands.

"What? You're kidding," he said, sitting up again.

"Of course you are. You found the body. And you were off duty. No way are you going anywhere near it from now on."

"Yes but–"

"Who were you with earlier on before going home and stopping off at Ileana's place on the way?"

Mal drew a deep breath. "James Palmer, Shifty Taylor–"

"Real names please."

"Thomas Taylor, Philip Bingley, Weas – er David Anders, Craig ... I don't his surname–"

"Get it by tomorrow. Is that all?"

"And my best mate, Boris Attwood."

The DI raised her head sharply from her note-making. There was a short pause before she continued.

"Where were you this evening?"

"A few bars. Then we went onto the Zone."

"Which bars?"

Mal looked blearily blank.

The DI sighed. "Oh never mind. You can come in early tomorrow and make a detailed statement."

Mal groaned again. The DI ignored this and barked out another question.

"Were all..." she looked down at her notes, counting names. "...all seven of you together all evening?"

"Yes. Well, no. Boris was late getting to the bar. But he's always late."

"How late?"

Mal sighed, yawned and rested his head on one hand.

"An hour or so?"

"Buck up, Mal. I want to get home to bed too, you know. Look, tell me again, and quickly. Why didn't you call it in instead of going up alone off-duty? Especially when it looked like the stair lights had been taken out."

The young officer appeared to gather himself and he spoke more clearly.

"Her flat lights were on. They never usually were. I just thought, if she needed help ... you know. I felt sorry for her. No friends or family apparently, a foreigner in this country, stuck up in that little bedsit. I was always walking past on the way to and from the bars along the canal. I just thought if she needed help ... you know."

"She was a pretty girl. Did you fancy her?"

Mal looked surprised; surprised apparently that a woman in her fifties would raise such a matter with him, a young male officer. He smiled in an embarrassed fashion.

"Dunno," he said looking down at his lap.

"Mal, you're a police officer. Don't play the ignorant clod with me. You know the score. This is a murder investigation. Nothing is out of bounds. Nothing, OK? So, did you fancy her?"

"I suppose so. But she was ... you know."

"No, I don't know. You tell me."

"She was ... I suppose ... a bit odd. There was something up with her anyway. Yeah, she was pretty, and if I'd met her in a club or something, then yeah, I'd've fancied her. But these people that report threats and then there's no evidence, well you have to wonder about them. And she was so cagey about everything. I still don't see why I can't work on the case though."

"Out of the question."

"But–"

"You bloody know why. The place'll be crawling with your DNA and fingerprints for a start."

"Well, if it wasn't, that'd be even more odd, wouldn't it?" Mal asked. "I mean, I'd already been there a few times, and I didn't go up there tonight actually expecting to find anything. I just thought I'd better, just in case."

"Quite possibly. But anyway *she's dead*. The poor girl is dead. Just twenty-four, she'd only recently come to this country to work and this happens to her. There's obviously going to be pressure from her country of origin to solve this. We've got to do our best to find the killer and not cloud the whole thing by letting you back on the case; not provide any opportunity for some clever dick defence counsel to claim any tampering with the scene or the evidence by an officer who blundered into the crime scene when he was off-duty."

Mal looked glum. "If I'd been there a bit earlier, I might have saved her. Then I'd have been a hero not a hindrance."

"Quite possibly," the DI said again. "But the fact is you didn't save her. Look, it's late. You must be tired. I know I am. And you'd been drinking. Go home, and in the morning you'll see it's the only way."

It was nearly two am. Mal's little terraced house a few streets away from the canal beckoned, and he was due back in at nine. He'd better take that advice at least.

"OK." Mal yawned. "Thank God it's just a half day tomorrow."

"Me too. For once. Go on. Off you go then."

"Night then, ma'am."

Mal rose from his chair and shambled out. His boss, half smiling, shook her head after him.

Chapter 3

EMOTIONS. So difficult to pin down, to define, to put into words. Even to find some reasonable explanation for. The physical manifestations were simpler to understand. They were there whether you liked it or not; the thumping heart, the pounding of the blood pulsing and hammering at the ear-drums, the slight shake to the hands, the seizing up of the facial muscles rendering even a weak smile impossible.

The cause of all this turmoil was standing some yards away with another younger woman peering down at some tawdry objects on one of the stalls. For heaven's sake, after two failed marriages and at his age, such things shouldn't affect him.

A memory, unbidden, assailed Guy Attwood, drawn from the depths of his brain by the sight of the woman. A magistrates' court some twenty-five or more years ago, sunbeams slanting through the rather begrimed windows set high in the wall, falling on dusty surfaces, onto Guy's notes before him.

The sounds of the fete faded into the background, as the fuzzy, grainy memory took over. Guy, a young solicitor, mid-twenties, watched while a uniformed WPC, faired-haired, to him intoxicatingly pretty and also mid-twenties, addressed the magistrates.

"Plainly the defendant is not present."

The police officer glanced over at Guy, archly, then back to the magistrates.

"No doubt Mr Attwood can enlighten the court as to whether there is any good reason."

"Well, Mr Attwood?" said the chairman of the magistrates.

Guy smiled. "Your Worships. Indeed I can explain..."

The image dissolved as Guy took a clumsy swig of his warm beer and narrowly missed spilling a quantity of it over his shirt front. He carried on regarding the woman. Were people really able to sense that they were being stared at? It sometimes seemed so. Suddenly, as if being controlled by an unseen puppet master, she turned her head and was looking directly at Guy and he was powerless to break the eye contact.

He was saved by his daughter, a young teacher at the mid-Hertfordshire primary school where the fête was taking place this early summer weekend. Without warning, she was next to him, asking him if he wanted to go and sit down with her for five minutes in the beer tent while she took a breather. Guy wondered if it would be rude just to march off, to not walk over and at least say hello to the woman. Should he? But he couldn't actually even remember her name and–

"Come on, Dad," said Andrea, already striding away, therefore he had no choice than to follow.

Guy bought his daughter an orange juice and a filled roll for both of them. He sat down and peered around.

"Your mother's not here is she?"

"Don't worry, Dad," Andrea laughed, "she's had to go to some event or other with Desmond."

Demon Desmond, thought Guy, the man who had nicked his first wife and split up his family. Desmond, so successful in his various business enterprises, so much more able to provide for Guy's wife and children. Affluenza seemed to have spread through his life like a ruddy virus.

His daughter continued: "They were driven off this morning; by Paul of course."

"Oh, Paul. Does he still dote on her? You know, moon at her like a love-sick Labrador?"

"Well, love-sick pit bull more like."

"I can't think why they need a driver at all. Can't they drive themselves? They're not disabled, are they."

"Dad, you don't realise. Mum is a woman of substance these days, with her charitable foundation, her public appearances and so on. She needs the driving time to ... get her paperwork in order, powder her nose. That sort of thing."

Guy shook his head.

"She's even got a Wikipedia entry," said Andrea.

"Wow. I wonder who put that up!"

"Well, he might have." They were both talking about Desmond.

"For hubris, that takes some beating."

"You're in it."

"What? What did I do to deserve that? I'll have to alter it immediately."

"Well, you *were* married to her once. And you're a senior university lecturer. You're obviously worthy of some mention. You might even have your own entry."

"I very much doubt it."

"You've written a few books."

"Yes, with a readership in the hundreds. On a very obscure subject most people haven't even heard of."

"All the same, one of your loyal students may have created an entry. You should Google yourself."

"That seems a bit sick to me. A bit sad."

"But anyway, Mum's foundation raises millions. It's a very good cause."

"Remind me what it is again."

"Deprived inner-city children. Befriending them, providing sports coaching, other recreational facilities, housing where necessary, education, counselling them towards coming out of these awful gangs they feel are their only option. Ultimately enabling them to have proper lives."

"Yes. Of course, it's very – valuable. Very creditable." And I wonder how far she'd get without Desmond's billions, Guy thought. "So what else are you up to today?"

"Boris might come along later."

"Oh good. It's months since I've heard from him. He's OK presumably."

"More than." And they chatted on about family things, Boris's various girlfriends and escapades, his promotion that Guy knew nothing about.

"You should come and visit more often," said Andrea.

"You're right. But, you know. There's nowhere to stay usually except some grotty chain hotel and … I don't know."

"Well, you can always have a guest suite at our place."

Guy took a swig of beer.

"Oh yeah, Mansion Desmond! How much longer are you going to live there?"

"Not sure. With my own flat there, it's uber convenient."

"Have you and Leo decided whether to get hitched yet?"

"There's no hurry." Andrea smiled wickedly. "You could doss down at Boris's."

"What? Bacteria Central? Doss is the word."

A child ran up to the table.

"Miss Attwood, it's the majorettes in fifteen minutes."

"Thanks. I'll be there."

The child ran off.

Conversation flagged. Guy mopped his brow and, from the relative cool of the tent, cast about among the crowd outside in the sunshine.

"Andrea, who's that woman over there? Eating an ice cream."

Andrea looked. "Dunno," she said. "Looks like she's here with a parent."

"Do you know the parent?"

"Of course. I know all the parents. Why? Do you know the woman?"

"Well, yes, a bit but … no, not really. Erm…"

ANDREA regarded her father with a half-smile. His second marriage had ended in divorce a year ago and, as far as she knew, he wasn't dating. She had noticed him gazing at the woman when she went to purloin him for a quick chat. And the woman staring back. She shook her head. It would do no harm.

"Come on, I'll take you over there. The parent is Janice Weeks and her son's in the choir. They're due to sing soon. You like choral music, don't you?"

AS GUY was being reintroduced to the woman at the school fête while trying to still the hammering of his heart and convey an appropriate level of interest in her without appearing to be creepily infatuated with her, his son Boris was once again at a canal-side bar with his friend Malcolm. They were both nursing massive hangovers, the process being helped along by a few hairs of the dog, and they were disjointedly discussing what to do tonight.

"You should throw a party," said Mal.

"What at our place? No chance. Have you seen the state of it lately?"

"No one cares about that. Anyway, it'd just get messed up and have to be cleared up again."

"Why don't you throw one then?"

"Get stuffed! I *own* my house. You should buy something. It's nuts paying rent. Your dad's loaded. Why don't you get him to buy you a nice little pad?"

"He's not my father, thanks."

"We could go to that new club that's just opened."

"I s'pose. Yeah, might be good. Isn't it a girls' free-entry night tonight?"

"What? On a Saturday?"

"Is it Women's Something-Or-Other Day today?" said Boris.

"Could be some sort of empowerment thing. Feminism. You know."

"Oh. Give that a miss then perhaps."

"It's Potato Face's birthday party tonight, isn't it? We could crash that."

"You know his parents always hover about. Not surprising I s'pose after what happened at the last one. Anyway, how's that case going? You know. The Romanian girl you found?"

"You know I'm off it." Mal sipped his lager.

"Yeah, but you must hear stuff."

"Just bits and pieces."

"Such as?"

"Not much considering it's not even been twenty-four hours. Preliminary; bloke's DNA was found at her flat. We didn't know she had any boyfriend or anything when she was alive. That's it really. It seems likely that whoever bumped her off got disturbed."

"Why do you think that then?"

"*I* don't think anything. *I'm* not allowed to think anything. It's just what's going around. Why d'you want to know anyway?"

"I'm interested. It's been in the newspapers."

"What about your real dad?"

"What about him?"

"Helping you out to buy a house."

"Haven't seen much of him lately. You didn't say why they think the person was disturbed."

"I told you before. The lights were on. That's why I went up there. And the doors were open. Like someone had to get away quickly without the time to shut the place up properly. What about your real dad? Couldn't he give you some cash to get a place of your own?"

"He's not that flush I don't think. Certainly not enough to buy a house around here. Outer Mongolia maybe. He's staying here this weekend."

"You've heard of a mortgage presumably. Why not ask him for a deposit?"

"Couldn't. He's only just got divorced."

"You seeing him?"

"Might. Tomorrow maybe. Duty meeting. And I'll get bought lunch."

"So what shall we do tonight then?"

Chapter 4

GUY awoke suddenly. His room was on the ground floor and some sort of noise from the hotel car park had disturbed him. A car door slamming maybe? He wasn't sure. He gently pulled his iPhone from the bedside table, conscious of, in fact in truth in complete awe of, the sleeping form beside him. Checking the time, it was only four-thirty in the morning. Though by this hour the sun would be up, very little light penetrated the thick hotel curtains.

In the darkness, the figure beside him stirred and grumbled. Guy's stomach rumbled but he smiled to himself, still marvelling at the turn of events. He pulled the woman to him and, without waking, she wound her legs around him. Seldom did one feel so contented and relaxed and Guy drifted off to sleep again.

BREAKFAST was a different matter however. Somehow or other, in between making love once they'd both woken up three hours later and sitting down in the restaurant looking at the menu (eggs this, eggs that), a certain stiffness had overtaken them.

His companion hadn't really wanted to have breakfast. She was all for leaving and going home once she was dressed, but she'd obviously noted his hurt expression and relented. It hadn't helped that he'd had to explain carefully to the young waitress that only he was booked in at the hotel with breakfast included, and that he wanted the lady's breakfast charged to his account. The waitress had raised a knowing eyebrow quite unnecessarily, unprofessionally even, Guy had thought. She sashayed off with their order.

"So, you're back off to Lincoln today then?" she said to Guy brightly and he couldn't help feeling that she was relieved that that was the case.

"Well, yes. Quite a bit later. I'm hoping to go out for a pub lunch with Andrea and Boris. Then," he sighed, "I'll leave it a bit before actually driving back. Perhaps I'll go and brave the wilds of Boris's rented house for an hour or so. If I don't stay too long, hopefully I won't catch anything."

The woman picked at her scrambled eggs and asked about his children, most especially Boris. Guy, tucking into his full English with some relish, answered her vaguely. Living alone, he could rarely be bothered to make a decent fry-up in the mornings, even at weekends.

At length, she took a swig of the by now tepid coffee and looked moodily at him.

"I'm surprised that you remembered me really," she said.

"Of course I remembered you." He half smiled. "You were a complete obsession for me. That tight uniform, those sidelong looks. I…" sometimes honesty was the best policy and he so hoped that she'd want to see him again, "…I was totally hooked on you."

"Goodness. I'd no idea."

"No, probably not," Guy sighed. "Well, you look just as gorgeous to me now as you did then."

"That's very sweet," she said, smiling. "So why did you go off and move to the wilds of Lincolnshire? You seemed to disappear once for a year or so ages ago and then again a bit later, apparently permanently."

They had had little chance to catch up last night. He had intended to go out with Andrea and Boris but, once he'd been re-introduced to the woman, he hadn't been able to tear himself away from her. Boris hadn't turned up at the school fête anyway and Andrea had wanted to go for a meal with Leo and some friends. With no reason not to, he'd suggested to the woman having dinner together and she'd agreed. They had arranged for her to come to his hotel, meet him in the bar at about eight in the evening and they'd decide where to go from there.

However she'd arrived quite a bit earlier than agreed and he hadn't even showered when she called him. It was a warm evening and his ground floor room had French windows out onto a small, pleasant, west-facing veranda with a table and chairs, therefore he'd suggested that she came and waited for him there. He had called reception for someone to take her there, at the same time ordering a bottle of chilled sparkling white wine to be brought for her consumption.

As soon as possible he had joined her. They had talked a little, but the evening was quiet and still and warm and relaxing. He had assumed that his capacity as a seducer, such as it had ever existed, was entirely spent by now. Yet as he sat companionably with this woman whom he had so admired, nay lusted after, in his twenties, his longing and yearning for her seemed to infect her too and they'd never made it to any restaurant that evening. Their love-making had lasted hours and hours, then she had fallen asleep and he couldn't even call for room service to bring him something to eat.

Consequently he was famished this morning. Responding to her question, he said:

"After my first marriage imploded, I decided on a complete change and thought I'd try lecturing. The job happened to be in Lincoln but I like it there now. It's quite civilised you know. It's a lovely city."

His breakfast companion nodded and toyed with her toast and marmalade. She then downed the rest of her coffee in one and said she had a difficult case on at the moment with international overtones.

"And I may have to attend a post-mortem a bit later."

"Oh. How grisly."

"Sorry. I should've thought. The DCI's away on holiday so the job falls to me. I'd better be off. Sunday or not, I've got to work today."

She stood up, looking slightly evasive.

"Oh, well. Bye then." Guy stood too, pushing back his chair. He opened his mouth to say something, then hesitated. "Er–"

"I'll – er – call you," she said.

And Detective Inspector Roz Benedict stood up and walked out of the hotel restaurant, leaving Guy to stare wistfully after her.

GUY switched on his car radio as his classic Jag joined the traffic on the A1 Northbound. The weather forecast was just ending.

"It's one minute past six this Sunday evening," said the announcer. Good. He should be home by eight. *"An update of traffic news is coming up in a moment. Before that, let's have a round-up of the latest local news."*

The background introductory music reached a peak and Guy listened indifferently.

"Hatford Police have issued the name of the Romanian girl murdered on Friday evening in her flat in Manor Road, Hatford. She's been named as Ileana Bratianu."

Guy briefly took his eyes off the road and looked down at the radio. He turned up the volume, face serious.

"Her family in Romania have been contacted. The murder is thought to have taken place about nine-thirty Friday evening. Detective Inspector Roz Benedict of Hatford Police appealed for anyone with information to come forward."

Guy's eyes widened. There was a brief pause in the news-reading.

"In other news, the date has been announced for–"

GUY switched off the radio, frowning.

Chapter 5

DESMOND watched his wife Liz across the restaurant table. It was a nuisance. He'd rather have had a quiet day and let Liz go off shopping if she'd wanted to.

They were due to attend a black tie event at the Intercontinental London Park Lane Hotel this evening, an event arranged by the Russo-British Chamber of Commerce. But this other couple were in town too this weekend, and Desmond and Liz couldn't really get out of meeting them for lunch.

Liz, sitting opposite, chatting happily to the MD of a regional wine merchants from Cambridge, looked sexy though smart in a tight fitting new dress bought last weekend on a trip to London; a treat for his darling Liz; shopping, then a show and a late dinner with friends. A stay at the Savoy - nothing too fancy - and a drinks party the following lunchtime before being driven home by their factotum Paul who had spent the Saturday night with relatives in the East End, as he was this weekend.

Two weekends in a row in London were quite enough.

Liz's fair hair was newly styled; her ruby necklace and matching drop earrings provided some sparkle. Her skin was radiant still, like a young girl's; her chin firm. And no cosmetic surgical input at all.

She was as gorgeous as the moment he'd first set eyes on her and had decided she had to be his. Having already made his first hundred million, it hadn't been difficult to sweep her off her feet and dazzle her with what he had to offer. Considerably more than that average solicitor she'd been married to.

A pity to break up a marriage, of course, but he'd done his very best for her children since then. He was looking forward to putting on a major send-off for their daughter Andrea when she and her intended decided to eventually get spliced.

Andrea, an angelic child, was by far the easier of the two children to get on with and she seemed to settle immediately, aged eight, into the new set up. A six-year-old Boris had been more difficult. Still, Desmond had convinced himself that now, at least, they had a reasonable relationship. Since Boris had left home.

He and Liz had unfortunately never had any children together, nevertheless Desmond felt every bit the father of her two and was glad he'd supported generous contact for Guy to see them.

He knew how to handle people, and that trying to come between a father and his children would have been a bad ploy, liable to backfire in the end and have the opposite result to that intended. And above all he wanted Liz to be happy and not have to endure any unpleasantness or difficulty.

Desmond coughed, as the wine merchant's wife looked pointedly at him to respond to her last boring comment.

He caught Liz's eye and her veiled sympathetic glance at him, and he knew he would do literally anything for her.

AT the same moment that Desmond was thinking about Boris, Guy was being let into Boris's shared house by another young man who looked as though he'd just been brought back from the dead on a mortuary slab; pale, sniffing and swaying, squinting and frowning at Guy.

Guy had knocked on the door for a full five minutes, initially gently, but eventually fairly violently until this apparition had materialised. The young man coughed and gestured weakly up the stairs and left Guy to find Boris's room himself.

The bedroom door was half open and Guy recognised Boris's guitar leaning up against the far wall. Putting his head round the door, he saw that it was indeed Boris in the bed, snoring away. He sighed.

The duvet and pillows were without covers, presumably worked off, as was the undersheet, over a number of weeks' wriggling and writhing while Boris slept. The bottom sheet, pillows, duvet and covers had been turned and turned repeatedly. The result was a nest-like, jumbled structure taking up one third of the bare mattress into which Boris must have twisted and curled himself on arriving home at some point last night from a serious clubbing session.

Guy shook his head. How Boris managed to turn himself out in a smart suit every day and go to London where he worked, apparently successfully, in asset-management, was a complete mystery. Guy knew how difficult it was to rouse Boris at the best of times. He cursed under his breath; he'd booked the table for one-thirty for himself, Boris and Andrea and he didn't want to keep Andrea waiting.

But, as ever, he wouldn't take Boris to task. They'd had such a hard time having two children that he and Liz had never been heavy parents.

Liz, beautiful and sexy though she was, had nevertheless suffered an early menopause. When this unthinkable event had been threatened, they'd both sunk every penny they could scrape together into IVF and a number of apparently 'viable' embryos had resulted. The first several to be used had given rise to the birth of sweet, perfect little Andrea and they had felt that it was essential to get on and have the second child without delay though by this time they were told that the remaining frozen embryos were not of the very best quality. They'd gone ahead anyway, and the second child to be born they'd named Boris after a great-grandfather of Liz's.

Guy had no idea how much Desmond knew of any of the early difficulties. Hopefully not everything.

Guy hadn't really blamed Liz when she went off with Demon Desmond. They'd been supremely hard up after all the scrimping and re-mortgages that had financed the IVF and other problems. In fact, he didn't believe that's what had caused her to leave. He knew it had been a huge blow to Liz's confidence, her womanliness, to have lost the use of her ovaries so early on and to have had to resort to assisted methods of reproduction.

She had been easy prey at the time to Desmond's wealth and overtures. Guy realised that, in truth, he had become pretty negligent of the marriage by then after all the huge stresses they'd been through. He was just about surviving himself.

It had all happened in a blur when Liz had suddenly announced her own and the children's impending departures to live with this hyper-energetic entrepreneur in his big, flash, ostentatious modern house that Guy had noticed when he passed it sometimes on the way to court.

Guy, not wanting to cause a fuss for the children, had gone along with it all without protest. They'd sold their house and he'd been allowed to keep the minuscule net proceeds with which he'd bought his first flat in Lincoln, a dowdy maisonette. However, it had three bedrooms so he was able to have the kids to stay.

And in Lincoln he'd gradually rebuilt his life. Despite how difficult it was for him, he made the effort to remain on good terms with Liz, though he secretly loathed Desmond. And he'd watched as Desmond had become more and more successful. At least Liz and Andrea seemed happy, while Boris was - well, Boris. He didn't clash openly with Desmond, but Guy knew they'd never had a comfortable relationship.

Liz, when he saw her, was as beautiful as ever. The HRT must have continued to keep any signs of ageing at bay very well.

Guy looked down now at this Boris, smiled and commenced the well-rehearsed routine of reviving him sufficient to struggle into some clothes and face a pub meal this warm Saturday lunchtime.

Chapter 6

"DIDN'T expect to see you back so soon, Dad," Andrea said, as soon as they were seated. "This wouldn't have anything to do with ... you know."

"Not sure I do know," Guy replied coyly. "You tell me."

"Oh, Dad! I saw you go off with her last Saturday and then the next day you were all dreamy. You spending the weekend with her?"

"Steady on. A father's allowed a little privacy surely."

In fact, though, it was rather a sore subject with him. They'd arranged to meet this weekend, but Roz had been doing something on the Friday evening and she hadn't wanted him to go straight to her house and await her return. She'd said outright that that was a bit too cosy for so soon.

Hence, he'd passed the Friday night in another ruddy miserable chain hotel so that he could spend most of the Saturday with Andrea and Boris. Roz, of course, was working again. It was very awkward since he now had his re-packed case in his car and nowhere to shower before this evening. They were having a meal tonight at her house and he was staying the night, which was something. He must've scored reasonably highly with her last weekend.

"You've gone all dreamy again." Before he could open his mouth to protest, Andrea went on: "A DI as well, isn't she?"

"DI?" said Boris. "You mean she's a lady police person. Or whatever." He was still a tad bleary. And he was puffing away at one of those awful electronic cigarettes. To get off the subject of Roz, Guy said to Boris:

"What's with the fags? You've never smoked before."

"It's cool to vape. And nicotine gets the brain moving, fires up the neurons. Everyone does it." He exhaled in Guy's direction. "And no nasty carcinogens either with these."

"I'm not so sure," said Guy. "And nicotine's highly addictive. You should try to keep it to a minimum."

"Don't be so anal. I only do it socially."

"Well, I'm flattered you regard meeting me as a social event, although you don't need to impress me, Boris."

But by now, Boris was looking down at his smart phone, his thumbs working away across the small screen. To pass the time, Guy made desultory conversation with Andrea.

"Your mother around this weekend?" he asked.

"No. They've gone to London again for some fancy do. It'll give Mum a shopping opportunity. And Paul's taking them of course. I suppose it'll give *him* a chance to catch up with his mates in gangland."

"Do you really think so? I mean that he has gangland connections?"

"Well, I do wonder. And you must admit that he has that air about him of a person who, shall we say, fixes things."

"Yes. I just assumed hitherto it was holiday bookings, dog kennels, plumbers. Those sorts of things."

"Maybe. But I'd prefer to have him on my side in a crisis."

Guy sipped his beer.

"So, no wedding bells this year?"

Andrea sighed and her expression changed, from sardonic to rather glum.

"Well, there's some light pressure in that direction. Not to mention keen anticipation of the patter of tiny feet."

"Sorry. I didn't mean to add to it. Just making conversation really. And of course I see so little of you and Boris."

"I don't really feel ready for kids yet. And especially not giving up work. I've only been qualified five minutes."

"Obviously it's up to you and only you. But you don't have to give up work when you have children these days. And it's not as though you're going to be hard up. I assume Desmond is grooming Leo for even greater things."

"I expect so. Keep it in the family, eh?"

"You do like him though, don't you?" said Guy, his brow wrinkled. "Leo? I mean, love him of course. I'd hate to think of you drifting into marriage because that's what everyone else wanted. And the baby production line."

"Oh yes. It's just ... I sometimes think it'd be simpler if I'd met him at uni for instance than at one of Desmond's events. But it wasn't like it was arranged or anything. Well, not as far as I know. We just hit it off straight away and–"

She was interrupted by Boris.

"Sod it." He looked up. To the others' questioning looks, he said: "My mate's got to work tonight. We were supposed to go clubbing. I'll just have to go to this party that's on instead."

"How terrible for you," said Andrea.

Boris looked at his father. "My mate's a DC. Probably knows your DI."

"Really," said Guy. "Shall we order now?"

Chapter 7

"THE soufflés'll be another couple of minutes." Roz paused and looked across the table at Guy. "So, you write books?"

"Er, yes. How'd you know?"

"Internet."

"Oh. Is nothing secret anymore?" Guy put his head on one side. "So you'll know they're not exactly mainstream. Not of interest to your average reader."

"Still, they've been published. That's an achievement in itself, isn't it?"

"They have. But I suppose there isn't a lot of competition in the field. They're mainly read by law students and a few enthusiasts. They're not going to make my fortune."

"I'd like to take a look at one."

Guy laughed. "I doubt if you would actually. If you suffer from insomnia, they might help."

Roz jumped up without answering.

"Oops. I'd better get the soufflés before they're ruined."

She quickly returned with a tray bearing two plates and a small jug of cream and sat down again.

Guy picked up his spoon and looked across at Roz.

"This is simply a brilliant meal."

He took a spoonful.

"This soufflé is stunning." He was impressed by the effort she must have made. The house was spotless, the dinner table perfectly laid though, by now on the pudding, they'd messed it up quite a lot and the candles were guttering. "Hmm. It's delicious. Did you make it?" The question was superfluous and he wished he hadn't asked when she replied:

"Did I hell! My cleaning lady's a great cook. She just left it all for me to put in the oven."

"Oh," said Guy, rather disappointed. Luckily he'd nearly finished the soufflé because it wasn't quite so appealing as he pictured an overweight, pinafored, red-faced, sweating, unkempt cleaner toiling in the kitchen.

“She’s Bulgarian,” Roz informed him.

“Really.”

“Yes. Bloody hard worker. Do you have any East European blood in your family?”

It seemed an odd question. “Don't think so. Why do you ask?” he said.

“It’s just your son’s name. Boris. I just wondered.”

“Oh. It was a family name of Liz’s.”

“Maybe she does then.”

“Maybe she does what?”

“Come from East European stock.”

“Not so far as I’m aware.”

He felt as though he was being grilled. She’d done this last Saturday and over breakfast on Sunday. Perhaps due to her job it had become second nature even when not working. Nevertheless, it was rather irritating. He must’ve looked peeved since she apologised.

“Sorry. Force of habit I suppose. It’s just that I think your Boris is friendly with one of my officers. Oh, and I’m working on a case at the moment involving a murdered East European girl.”

“What, another Bulgarian?”

“No. She was Romanian.”

Guy was silent. He put down his spoon and raised and peered into his wine glass.

Roz obviously decided to drop the subject.

“So,” she said, “when you took your year off, was it some sort of legal sabbatical? A prelude to your university career perhaps?”

“Not exactly.” Guy’s expression was closed. He took a sip of wine.

“Right then,” said Roz. “Would you like coffee? A liqueur?”

“Only if you’re having either.”

Roz got up from the table and came and stood next to Guy. She put one hand on his shoulder. He relaxed and smiled up at her, glad that he’d braved the shambles of Boris’s bathroom and showered earlier on.

"I'm not bothered," she said. "Shall we go up?"

GUY was clattering about in Roz's kitchen. She hadn't wanted to clear up the next morning, saying the cleaner would do it.

"You should ask the cleaner to move in with you," Guy had said and Roz had laughed.

She hadn't wanted to make breakfast either, therefore, after loading and starting the dishwasher, Guy was frying bacon and eggs for them. This hadn't been how he'd imagined it but at least he was getting to spend the day with her today. And she came up behind him, put her arms around his waist and nibbled at his ear.

"You get an extra hash brown for that," he said and, turning round, he kissed her.

"Shall we spend the morning in bed after breakfast?" she said.

"Excellent idea. I'll take the plates through."

SEATED at a table outside one of the canal-side bars, Guy was quite peckish again. It had been Roz's idea to come here for a late lunchtime drink. They hadn't got out of bed until gone two and Roz said she wasn't really hungry. He persuaded her to have a soup and roll. He'd feel like a glutton, tucking into anything substantial while she sat and watched.

Food was still being served. The board said it was served all day until ten-thirty. The bars were heaving. These places must make a packet. No wonder Demon Desmond, in the so-called hospitality industry as he was, had made a fortune sufficient to enable the family to now reside in an enormous refurbished Georgian mansion set in three hundred acres. Andrea was able to ride, use the gym, be waited on hand and foot; and she had her own self-contained flat within the house somewhere, though Guy had never visited her there.

Guy secretly applauded the fact that Boris had broken loose, took nothing from Desmond and arranged his life to suit himself. Though he always had.

"Quite a few of my officers come down here," Roz was

saying, looking around as though she expected she might spot a gaggle of them now. "I told you one of my officers was friendly with your Boris. That rather surprised me."

"Oh? Why?"

"Well. Your daughter, Andrea, from what I've seen of her through my niece's children being at the school where she teaches, I mean, she speaks and acts like a deb or something. You know, a young lady. Kind of a society person."

"So?" He'd never really thought this about Andrea but then, to him, she was just his daughter.

"Well, she must have been to public school; boarding school even. I just thought, if Boris was privately educated too, I wonder how he and my officer would have got to know one another. My officer said they were old school friends and my officer's certainly not out of the top drawer."

"Boris insisted on going to the Sixth Form College once he'd done GCSEs. Perhaps that's where they met. He still did well though. He got into Cambridge and he's got a good job now."

"They must both have good genes then," she said looking pointedly at his crotch.

"Roz!" he said, putting his fork down and taking her hand. He smiled. "You're insatiable."

"D'you mind?"

"Course not." He kissed her hand and she fondled his leg. He wanted to go back to bed with her right now and he could feel the adrenaline starting to flow, making him tingle in unsuitable places, inconveniently in public. He cleared his throat. "Go on. Divert me. Tell me something else about your work."

"Oh. Right," said Roz, swallowing. "Yes. Good idea. Well, an odd thing's come up with this Romanian murder victim I was telling you about. She was bumped off in her little rented studio flat. We know almost nothing about her but we found various men's DNA around the place. One of them was my officer. He'd been there before because she'd allegedly been receiving threats, and he actually found her dead, so that's not surprising."

"You mean Boris's friend?"

"Yes. And there was DNA from a strange man of Hispanic extraction we're unable to identify. But the odd thing was that the third man's DNA appeared to be from a sibling of the deceased."

"What? A brother? A Romanian man?"

"Well, yes, presumably, if he was her brother. And his DNA profile was East European."

"Oh."

Roz was peering at him. Yet again, he felt he was under minute scrutiny. His face, he was confident, probably conveyed nothing. Nonetheless, she knew he had been a criminal lawyer, a court advocate earlier on in his career. She'd be aware that solicitors and barristers trained themselves to give nothing away in court. No hint of nervousness, no reaction to a put-down from some judge or magistrate, no uncertainty if something unexpected arose. No sign of embarrassment allowed to leak into their features if they somehow showed themselves up.

What she'd said was certainly a passion-killer. Guy realised that he had pulled his hand away and he saw Roz shiver a little despite the warm sunshine. He wished she'd talked about something else. The pressures of the job, the avalanche of paperwork everyone laboured under these days. Promotion prospects. Anything.

Guy watched her. He thought he saw her face alter fractionally, showing uncertainty perhaps.

"Roz," he said. "I think it's best to be honest. I like you so very much. But you have this way of seeming to interrogate me, looking for some sort of reaction. That's what it feels like anyway. Perhaps you don't mean anything by it, but I don't like it. Actually, quite frankly, it's a little creepy. If we couldn't see each other again, I'd be very upset. Very upset indeed, but…"

He tailed off. *But what?* He was probably irreversibly hooked by now, powerless to cut loose, go back to Lincoln and forget her. He didn't think it was possible, and now he regretted what he'd just said. She might take him up on it and –

oh God, he wouldn't recover for ages.

Her expression however was deepening. He saw a vulnerability there and he found it very appealing indeed. Hard-nosed, sex-mad career woman was all very well, but a little femininity wouldn't go amiss either.

"I'm sorry, Guy. I didn't want to whinge about work in general. Of course I shouldn't be talking to you about the case at all. Or any case. It was just the East European thing and I wondered if anything had filtered through to you via Boris knowing my officer.

"I didn't mean – I didn't realise – it's just that I used to think about you so much, you know, before, when we'd see each other at court and so on. I knew you were married but ... And then you disappeared. And now you're back..."

Just as I felt too, Guy thought.

He saw her eyes had watered. "I only wanted to find out a bit about you," she was saying. "I wondered because of Boris's name if you had some East European connection and knew anything about the countries, the cultures et cetera." She sniffed. "God knows, my own life hasn't been big on relationships. No kids. Short, failed marriage. The odd romance. I haven't got much to tell. Yours seems to have been more eventful, that's all. We can still see each other again, can't we?"

Guy drew his chair close to hers and, despite their being in public, he folded his arms around her and felt her shudder a little.

"Of course we can," he whispered in her ear. And he knew he was at least ninety per cent in love with her already.

Chapter 8

IT WAS an infernal nuisance but it had to be borne every few weeks. After the trips to London two weekends running, Desmond could have done with a session in his study at home this Sunday evening, poring over the last month's figures. He looked sourly up at the exterior of the Magnolia Retirement Home, an immaculately kept, large, converted country house. And didn't it cost a packet.

Emerging from his new Range Rover, he walked into the building, greeted the receptionist and made off along a corridor to the right in the direction of his mother's room. Large suites on the ground floor cost an arm and a leg, but his mother insisted upon a view and a pair of French windows directly out into the garden.

Before long, he was seated in one of the comfortable armchairs, as was his mother. He opened one of the newspapers provided to the old woman by the home. She stared into space taking no notice of her son and Desmond looked at her coldly. At length, he roused himself.

"So how've you been, Mum?" he said with feigned cheerfulness. "Looking after you OK here are they?"

His mother ignored him. His peeved expression made no impression on her.

"All right," he said, "if you're not in a mood to talk, doesn't matter. We'll just sit here."

His Mother spoke at last. "Huh! You'd like that, wouldn't you. Sit and read the financial pages for half an hour and then bugger off to your so-called family. Or rather someone else's family."

Desmond rolled his eyes.

"What's brought this on again? I thought you'd got over that. We're a happy family. These things happen. Liz and I fell in love. The kids are doing well. I don't know why you have to keep bringing it up."

Mrs Madison's eyes narrowed, her features vindictive.

"Stealing another man's family from under his nose. Just because you're rich. You should be ashamed of yourself. Breaking up a family. Those little children not understanding why everything had to change."

"Mum, none of this does any good. Anyway, what about you? It's a lovely day. Why don't you go and sit outside with some of the others?"

"Weak in the head, most of them."

Desmond leaned over and held a carrier bag near his mother.

"OK. Here, I've brought you some novels. Andrea thought you might like to read them. She picked them especially."

Mrs Madison ignored the bag.

"The food's bloody horrible here," she said. "Swill."

"You've never complained about it before."

"Huh! While you and your fancy piece eat in the poshest, most expensive restaurants."

"Well, you can come out and have dinner with us any day in these so-called posh restaurants. You're more than welcome. And don't call her that. She's my wife."

"Your tart. Someone else's rightful wife. I'm not sitting at table with that slut."

"Suit yourself. It's your loss, not ours."

"The trouble and pain they had to go through to have those children, and you just made away with them. It's criminal. You always get what you want, don't you."

"Mum, I'm really sorry, but I can't see the point in continuing with this. I could easily be in the office now doing a bit of–"

"Yes, I know. Working. Work, work, work. Money, money, money."

Desmond stood up.

"OK, Mum. I think we've covered enough of our usual ground today. I'll be off then."

"Good riddance."

"Bye, Mum.

Desmond bent to kiss her. She shrugged him away. His

mouth tightened, and he straightened and walked out. He stood for a moment outside the closed door, head bowed disconsolately. A uniformed member of staff bustled towards him and stopped. Desmond looked up.

"Oh hello, Tina."

"I'm just about to look in on her. See if she's eaten her tea. Was she OK today?"

"So, so."

"Well, I say. Two visitors in one day. Lucky her."

"Oh yeah?"

"Yes. Her grandson came earlier. Boris isn't it?"

"That's right. It must be some time since he came."

"Ooh it is. But he's not a one to forget. Joking and making us all laugh. A breath of fresh air he is. He well cheered up your mother."

"Well, good," Desmond said blandly, turning his head away so that Tina wouldn't see the baleful expression that crossed his face.

"Hmm. I'd better go and see after her then."

"Yes of course. Er, thanks for all you and the others do for her."

"It's a pleasure, Mr Madison."

Desmond stood aside for Tina who opened the door and walked in.

"And how are we this evening Mrs Madison? I'll just clear your tea things up."

Tina closed the door. Desmond plodded off down the corridor.

GUY'S Jag found itself joining the traffic on the A1 northbound once again the following day. He'd set off early to get back from Hertfordshire to Lincoln in time for work. He was supposed to return last night. Somehow, though, he hadn't. When he and Roz had arrived home from the bar yesterday afternoon, they'd gone straight to bed and more or less stayed there.

Despite the early start, having to leave a sleepy, cuddly Roz in bed at five-thirty am, he felt fantastic. A day and a half of nearly non-stop sex left him fresh and fully spring-cleaned, pipes fully blown, mind and body flushed of all negative humours. And they had agreed to spend most of next weekend in bed too. There were definitely worse ways to occupy one's leisure time.

Yawning, he switched on his radio and found it was still tuned to the local Hertfordshire station. He always seemed to catch the end of the weather forecast. A blast of bland introductory music reached a peak as the announcer spoke.

"It's six-ten this Monday morning. We'll give you an update on traffic news in a moment. Before that, let's have a roundup of the latest local news."

Guy leaned forward keenly.

"A police spokesperson has stated that there have been fresh developments in the case of the murdered Romanian girl, Ileana Bratianu. It's expected that there may be a press conference later today or tomorrow, with a possible appeal for a witness to come forward.

"Police believe that a key person may hold ground-breaking information about the attack. The police haven't, however, revealed any details of who this person might be or what evidence he or she may be able to provide. We'll keep you posted as further information emerges."

More nameless musac filled the next few seconds.

Guy's face was pensive, serious, as he put his foot down and switched over to BBC Radio 4.

A FANTASTIC weekend had been partly spoiled, so when Guy's smart phone tinkled as he pulled into his drive in Lincoln and he saw it was Roz, his mood lifted. He smiled down at the phone as though Roz was actually there with him.

It was a text from Roz suggesting that they invite Andrea, Boris and their respective partners over for a meal next Friday or Saturday evening. He frowned; what about the weekend of carnal activity they'd planned? And what about Roz's seeming reluctance to get too involved? He texted back:

"How cosy is that?"

"I thought you'd like to spend some time with them as well as with me. And we have to eat sometime too!" came the response. He replied that he'd see what could be arranged.

He continued to smile as he walked away from his car. The Bulgarian cleaner would be working overtime.

Chapter 9

WHEN Roz entered the CID unit on Monday morning, she went straight to DCI Len Thompson's glass-walled room, seeing the light on and him in there. Knocking and entering, she said breathlessly:

"Wow, am I glad to see you back. Have a good break?"

"Hmm. Not sure I'll try singles holidays again. I thought a walking holiday might be safe enough from desperate ladies. It was OK till the après-hiking got going but then it just descended into a free-for-all."

"Doesn't sound so bad."

"Yes, well, I must've ticked the wrong age-group box. Anyway, I'll tell you later. Bring me up to speed on the Romanian case."

"Right. It appears to have been planned. The perp was obviously prepared to pick the exterior door lock and put the stair lights out. They're up quite high. Mind you, the murder and the entry into the flat were low-tech. Strangulation. And he just smashed his way into the flat."

"Low-tech perhaps. But both quick and effective. And not too messy."

"Noisy though. But the other flat occupiers work nights. Looks like poor Ileana went into the bathroom to try to hide. No one there to help her."

Len sighed.

"Hmm. No news on the Romanian brother?"

"Not so far. No record of his DNA on the NPC or the Hispanic guy's either. Nothing much from the Europol liaison officer. The family are saying they have no idea. They claim none of the sons have been to England. But it's a big family. Two children have emigrated to Australia, one's died and they've actually lost touch with a couple of the older children. Some of the rest are dispersed around Europe. They're not helping. And the parents are old, and it sounds like they're poorly educated. Upset naturally, but not really inquisitive about the murder."

"And nothing from the public over here either from what I've read."

"Nope. And the work colleagues' DNA and prints didn't match anything in the flat. We've not traced any friends or boyfriends. Mind you, she'd barely been in England a couple of months. We'll have to assume as usual that most of the prints and DNA were from shop assistants, previous occupiers and so on. And probably some from the Romanian brother but you know how difficult it is to lift DNA from fingerprints and it didn't seem worth it with no matches on the NPC."

"I was thinking that for the time being at least we should keep the Romanian brother to ourselves. Just in case it's misleading." Len flicked through the file as he spoke.

"Right, and of course he's likely to do a runner if we announce his existence to the world."

"Quite. And the Hispanic man looks like the strongest candidate to be the killer. The hair and sweat on her clothing and so on. Obviously there could be some other reason for that. But I think we should work on the Romanian family a bit more and the Romanian authorities before putting out information about a brother."

"No, you're right. We don't want to drown the public in too much information."

"I'm hoping for a few extra details on the Hispanic man. I'd say he's our best bet. We didn't check the ports and airports did we?"

"Not for the Hispanic man, we didn't, no. It seemed pointless. At any one time there may be a hundred thousand or more Spanish people living in the UK. And we've no idea what the man looks like. Plus his genetic makeup suggests he could be South American."

"Still..."

"I thought about checking arrivals and departures around that time, but the volume of movement is staggering. Just between here and Spain or Portugal, let alone the South American states. And the person may not be a Spanish citizen so he wouldn't show up in the figures. And he may have taken an indirect route via other countries. It just wasn't possible."

"What about the brother then? At least we've got a name."

"It's not an uncommon surname actually, Len. There are a lot of Bratianus in this country. And of course the brother may not use that surname. We've got a list of males named Bratianu who entered the country in the month before the murder and those who've left since the murder and we're working our way through them but it's a massive task. And as for approaching those who've lived in this country for any length of time, it's impossible. We haven't–"

Len waved away the idea. "I know, I know. Resources." He sighed. "OK. How about putting the press conference off until tomorrow?"

"Suits me," said Roz. "Right. See you later."

Roz backed out. Their quick-fire discussion had taken only a few minutes. This was how it always was; how Len liked it. He didn't like to hang about. Unmarried, as she was, he'd probably been in the office for hours already, getting on top of things. He'd just wanted a little flesh to apply to the bones and she'd efficiently provided that. As usual.

LATER the same day, Desmond drove into a parking space outside Hatford railway station and turned up the radio. He watched as commuters walked away from the station entrance.

"...And the dog has been reunited with his owners, none the worse for his ordeal."

The tone of the local radio station newsreader's voice was light-hearted. There was a few seconds' delay before he continued.

"Now for something more serious. The anticipated press conference regarding the murder of Romanian girl Ileana Bratianu failed to take place today. A police spokesman indicated that the conference will probably be re-scheduled for tomorrow. We'll bring you more news as it emerges."

Desmond craned his neck. Boris emerged from the station building and Desmond lowered the volume. Boris was walking past the Range Rover and back-tracked when he heard the horn sound. He bent down and peered into the car.

Desmond leaned over and opened the nearside door.

"Come on. Get in, mate. I'll give you a lift."

A series of combined expressions crossed Boris's face; surprise, suspicion, non-committal.

"Damned decent of you," he said without smiling.

"I happened to be passing."

Boris regarded Desmond, not in a friendly way.

"Hmm," he said as he curled himself into the front passenger seat.

Desmond backed out of the parking space and drove away through the commuter traffic.

"And I haven't seen you for some weeks," he said.

Boris shrugged.

Desmond checked his mirror and changed lanes.

"I visited Magnolia yesterday," he said.

"Oh yes?"

"Mum was her usual self. Charming as ever."

"Perhaps she doesn't like it, living in a residential care home."

Desmond laughed mirthlessly.

"I doubt that's the problem. But anyway, I understand you've been there yourself, entertaining the care assistants."

Boris stared ahead. "And?" he said.

"Well, I just wondered why."

"She's my grandmother."

"Actually she's not. Not really."

"She's the nearest thing I've got to a grandmother. I like going to see her."

"So much so that you haven't been near the place for six months as far as I know."

"Well then, I was overdue."

"Come on, Boris. Why now?"

"Why not now?"

"It just seems odd. That's all. You can't have much to discuss with her. Or her with you for that matter."

"She's lived in this town all her life. I like to find out about the family history. Course I do. What's wrong with that?"

Desmond pulled a face. "Nothing I suppose. But your mother and I can tell you all you want to know about that."

Boris was tight-lipped.

"And Guy I suppose."

"Gee thanks. I can talk to my own father. That's very generous of you."

"Boris, you know I didn't mean it that way. I just meant … that I wondered why you'd picked … just recently … to rake over the past."

Desmond changed down a gear as a junction approached. "Probably," he continued, "because of that I got the rough edge of her tongue yesterday about … things."

"Tough titty."

"Anyway, best you don't mention your visit to your mother. She's stressed enough as it is for the moment."

Boris twisted his head sharply and looked directly at his stepfather for the first time.

"Why's she stressed? What's the matter?"

"Oh, just the foundation, I imagine. It's huge now and getting harder to manage. *And* she's looking to expand all the more, open up new areas. I don't want her worried with anything else."

Boris didn't reply. He continued to stare at Desmond, his expression unreadable. If Desmond noticed, he didn't react.

Conversation between the two men stalled. Desmond turned into Boris's road and stopped at the house. The engine idled as Boris opened the nearside door and made to get out.

"Why not come round one evening soon," said Desmond, leaning towards Boris. "Make it really soon. Have a family meal together. It'd be nice. Haven't done that for ages."

Boris climbed out of the car and bent over.

"OK. We'll see," he said.

Slamming the door shut, he turned and walked through the front gate. Soon he was in the house. Had he turned back to wave to Desmond, he might have witnessed Desmond's steady, speculative gaze at his departing figure.

BORIS went straight to his room and, opening his laptop, he typed into the Google search box:

'Do children recover from epilepsy?'

From the results listed, he scrolled and clicked on:

'Childhood epilepsy syndrome'

He read and scrolled, stopping at the words:

'Severe syndromes may not respond to treatment. Others, called "benign", are likely to resolve and the symptoms disappear by the time the child reaches a certain age.'

He leaned back, going over the words several times, then lowered the screen and shook his head, staring pensively out of the window.

Chapter 10

THE pub near London Kings Cross station was crowded. It was early Tuesday evening, not long after knocking-off time. Office workers relaxed before tackling the commute home. Boris was propping up the bar with some others. The overhead TV showed the news at low volume and most people were ignoring it.

"Right, I'd better be off." He tossed back the rest of his drink and started to walk out, to desultory expressions of farewell. Glancing back, his exit was arrested by the words 'press conference' and 'Hatford murder'. The news presenter stood poised in half-profile towards the camera, holding his notes.

"In a press conference held earlier today regarding the death of the murdered Romanian girl, police issued a further appeal for witnesses to come forward."

Boris hurried back, grabbed the remote control from the bar and increased the volume. The TV screen zoomed to a recording of the press conference. A man stood at the front of the room and looked around as the coughing and fidgeting died down.

'Good afternoon. I am Detective Chief Inspector Thompson and my colleague here is Detective Inspector Benedict. We won't be taking questions today. The purpose of this conference is to appeal to the public once again to come forward and furnish any information they can, however tenuous, that might be connected to the murder of Ileana Bratianu who arrived from Romania in April this year to work in this country. She spoke good English and worked in a clerical capacity in a small travel firm in Hatford, Hertfordshire.'

The DCI looked down at his notes and continued.

'She lived in a rented flat in Manor Road, Hatford. The murder took place in the flat at about nine-thirty on the evening of Friday 10th June, eleven days ago. The cause of death was strangulation. I'll hand over now to Detective Inspector Benedict who has some further information.'

Boris watched avidly.

AT THE same time in his kitchen in Lincoln, Guy Attwood popped a meal in the microwave. His TV too was tuned to the early evening news. His small TV sat in the corner on the work surface and Guy stared at it and increased the volume.

Roz looked into the camera. Guy felt as though she was speaking directly to him and fought with himself to ignore the visions playing around in his head of their last few hours together yesterday.

'We have reason to believe that a man with a so-called Hispanic/Latino genetic makeup was involved in the murder. I'm about to list the possible characteristics of the person but these are merely generalisations and you should remember that all or none of them may actually apply to the individual himself. They are merely indications.'

Roz paused and sipped from a glass of water. Without notes, she continued.

'Such an individual could be of largely European ancestry but may have more recently resided in a South America country or a state towards the South of the United States of America or he may have some family connection to those locations. The man is likely to have dark hair and brown eyes and may be dark-skinned. He may have South-American-Indian facial features. He is likely to be aged mid-twenties to mid-forties. He may have a Spanish-sounding name and he may speak with an accent.'

Roz paused again.

'Anyone who knows of such an individual having had contact with the deceased or who may have seen or know of such a person in the vicinity of Manor Road, Hatford at around the date of the murder, Friday 10th June, is asked to come forward.'

Roz took a breath, looked down, then back at the camera.

'A further possibility is a man whose appearance and character fit some of the criteria I've mentioned and who was in the area for some days around the date of the murder and then disappeared. He may have used cash in shops rather than a debit or credit card. Please contact us if you are aware of any such person. A telephone number will be given out to the press and media at the end of this conference and the information given today is on our website dedicated to this

case which also shows a recent photograph of Ileana. The photograph, website address and contact telephone number will be shown immediately after the airing of this press conference. As my colleague indicated, we won't be taking questions. Thank you.'

Roz and Len turned and walked out. A couple of journalists shouted questions but they were ignored.

Guy stood looking at the screen open-mouthed.

Boris was standing too, watching the screen avidly. He became aware that his colleagues were examining him curiously. He collected himself.

"It's my home town they were talking about."

He smiled.

"And the lovely DI Benedict is my dad's girlfriend."

The colleagues cheered. Boris laughed, collected up his briefcase, raised his hand and this time walked out.

Chapter 11

ONCE again, Guy found himself on the A1 the following Friday afternoon, early so as to make Roz's house with a decent interval to spare before Boris and Andrea arrived for dinner. Saturday hadn't been possible for them.

The going tonight was rather slow and he turned on the radio, though happily there were no major traffic hold-ups. An announcer told listeners:

'The hot weather looks set to hold up for the weekend, largely countrywide. So if you're going away for the weekend, make sure you pack your bikinis girls. And your budgie-smugglers guys…'

Guy smiled and shook his head, in a good mood.

'Oh, and don't forget the sun cream. No major hold-ups on the roads. Full news and weather in half an hour. And here's the latest hit from…'

Guy switched off the radio, still smiling, and contemplated this evening. Initially sceptical about the idea, he was now quite pleased that this dinner had been arranged. He'd barely had anything to do with Leo, not least since the young man worked in a managerial capacity for Demon Desmond. And it would be interesting to see who Boris turned up with. As Roz said, he needed to spend some time with the kids.

HAVING been introduced to the Bulgarian cleaner Stefka, a pretty neat girl in her late twenties (a pinafore, yes, but cool and slender with no underarm stains), Guy shook her hand and said:

"My mouth's been watering all week. The meal you cooked us last week was stupendous."

Stefka was inclined to be bashful and blushed.

"Thank you," she said. "It's all on time Roz. Should be ready to serve like you said about eight-twenty."

"Great. Actually, I'd better go and shower," Guy told the women. "I'm not quite as early as I'd hoped."

Having showered and changed in record time, Guy rushed

to the front door as the bell rang.

Andrea and Leo were ahead of time. Guy hugged Andrea and shook hands with Leo.

"Hello," he said.

"Hi," said Leo. "So pleased to meet you again."

"Come on then," said Guy. "Come and meet Roz."

Andrea gave him a sly, teasing look.

"I've been eagerly anticipating this."

"Hey, you, watch it." Guy smiled indulgently at his daughter.

He led them into the sitting room and more introductions followed as Roz accepted the customary bottle of red wine proffered by Leo and poured everyone a welcoming glass of chilled sparkling white.

"I hope you all like a drop of fizz," she said. Guy helped her hand out the glasses.

As the flutes were chinked and the bubbles went up Guy's nose, he tried to avoid Andrea's slight smile and raised eyebrow. He was entitled to a private life, wasn't he?

Everyone sat down.

"Sorry we're a bit early," Andrea apologized.

"We thought we'd compensate for Boris," said Leo. He, Andrea and Guy all laughed and Andrea explained to Roz:

"His timekeeping is abominable. He's always late for everything."

"So I've heard," said Roz.

"Oh yes?"

"Er, one of my DCs is friendly with him. He's mentioned him."

"Oh." Andrea was still surprised. There was a pause. "Well, actually we knew that. Boris said. I'm just surprised such a detail got back to you."

Roz shrugged. "The police are human beings too, you know."

"Yes, of course."

If Andrea felt she'd been taken down a peg or two, she didn't especially show it. Nevertheless, there was a slightly uncomfortable pause. Guy, as the person in the middle, felt he should move things along.

"How's things at the firm then, Leo?"

"Can't grumble. Expanding exponentially actually. Des wants to get a foothold in Russia. We've already got a lot of interests in Eastern Europe and the Balkans. Russia's a different matter. It's–"

"The Balkans? Which countries?" Roz interrupted.

"Mainly those bordering the Black Sea. Bulgaria and Romania. Some wonderful under-exploited resorts on the Black Sea."

"Oh. That's interesting. As you probably know, we're investigating the murder of a Romanian girl here."

"Yes," said Leo. "It's a fascinating country. Lashings of history."

Guy looked at his watch.

"It's eight-thirty already. You know, I should have told Boris to turn up at seven, not eight. Then there might have been some chance he'd be here on time."

Stefka entered from the kitchen.

"Everything's ready. I don't want it to spoil," she said.

"Don't worry, Stefka," Roz told her. "Boris and his partner are bound to be here soon."

"OK. I'll keep it warm."

As Stefka retreated to the kitchen, the four of them talked on. Guy found Leo charming. He wasn't surprised Andrea had fallen for him. Leo referred frequently to "Des" and Guy wondered if Leo was Desmond's protégé. Perhaps that was the setup, with Andrea, and ultimately the whole business, being the prizes on offer. And for Andrea, there wouldn't be many men available who'd be able to keep her in the style to which she'd become accustomed.

He had plenty of time to make these speculations to himself and examine Andrea's and Leo's interaction since Boris was supremely late, something that might have been anticipated had Guy been thinking. As he'd said, he should have asked Boris to arrive at seven instead of eight. Then they might not have been sitting about at nearly nine o' clock trying to find things to say and getting more and more tipsy, as Stefka enquired with increasing urgency when they wanted the dinner served.

She was walking in again now, worry creasing her brow.

"The meal will probably be ruined if I don't serve it soon.

"Sorry, Stef," said Roz. "I shouldn't think it'll be much longer."

Stefka sighed. "OK. I'll turn the oven down a bit."

"I can't wait to meet Boris. I've heard so much about him. From my DC." Roz looked at Andrea. "I expect you and he look very much alike, being so close in ages."

Andrea turned to Leo, her eyebrows raised.

"Actually," he said, "I've seldom seen a sister and brother look less alike."

"Really!" said Roz.

"They've both got fair hair and blue eyes, but the resemblance ends there."

Andrea shrugged. " I've never thought about it. I've got tons of friends who look completely different from their brothers and sisters."

"Let me pour everyone another glass of this excellent bubbly," Guy said, "because I can't see the object of our deliberations arriving any time soon. Quite honestly, I think we ought to put Stefka out of her misery and let her serve up."

"All right," said Roz. "I suppose that's the best idea. Why don't you all go into the dining room then. I'll go and tell Stef."

In the dining room, Guy went to refill everyone's glasses.

"Thanks," said Leo. "I'm driving. I'll stick to water."

Despite the delay and the re-heating, the meal was delicious. The conversation flowed, Guy was happy to note, though the two empty seats aggravated him no end.

As the pudding was being served, Leo turned to Roz.

"Your job must be immensely exciting. Solving crimes all the time."

"Yeah, well, for 'exciting' read 'frustrating'. With some cases, a lot of it's pure luck. Hitting on the right chord by utter chance and actually getting somewhere. Take for instance this case–"

The front doorbell rang and Guy looked at his watch. "Christ. Half past nine. I should have known. I'm really sorry. Excuse me."

Guy left the room to let in Boris and his companion.

"Hi everyone. Siss," said Boris, swaying a little as he came into the dining room with a girl in full Goth regalia. "Pleased to meet you, Roz." He went and shook her hand and she looked up at him with an amused expression. "This is Poison." He gestured to the girl. "Great, isn't she."

"Hmm," said Guy, stony-faced. "You'd better sit down."

Boris sat clumsily opposite Roz who continued to smile at him, fascinated. Andrea and Leo seemed unfazed, resigned. Poison fluffed her black robes and sat down too.

Stefka came in bearing a tray. "I served your dinners and put them in the oven. I hope they're OK."

"I'm a vegan," said Poison.

Stefka looked uncertain.

Boris said, "I think we'll skip dinner if it's all the same to you."

"Boris!" said Guy. "That's exceedingly ru–"

"Don't worry," said Roz. "Have some wine."

"I'll just have water," said Poison. "But it has to be distilled."

Stefka walked out.

"Boris, could I talk to you for a moment," said Guy. "In the sitting room."

Boris stood and took a few paces unsteadily.

"Could we cadge a lift home?" he said to Leo. "We had to walk here. Ashully, I've had a bit to drink."

"No problem," said Leo.

And Boris followed Guy out, making a mock salute to Roz as he went.

"WHAT'S going on here, Boris?"

"What do you mean?"

"You know what I mean. Turning up here so late and with – that girl."

Boris shrugged elaborately. "You told me to bring someone. And I haven't got a girlfriend just now."

"How surprising! But why does that make you late?"

"I had to go out and find someone."

"When? Not tonight, surely?"

"Well, yes."

"So you don't even *know* her! Why someone like her then?"

"I had to go to a pub where the Goths hang out."

"But why?"

"Quite appropriate I thought. Goths." Boris laughed in a slightly unhinged way.

"Boris?"

"Anyway, the girls are such dogs, I knew I'd be able to pick one up there."

So this was modern male youth; his son referring to girls as 'dogs'. He hoped Boris didn't mean it. How long did this go on for, he wondered. Boris was twenty-four now. Would a thirty-four-year old Boris still be oversleeping and showing him up? But Boris, though independent with terminally atrocious time-keeping, wasn't normally so rude and uncooperative as this.

"Boris, have I done something to upset you?"

For a second, the drunken buffoon disappeared and Boris's eyes became steely. "Now what would that be then?"

"I don't know. Enlighten me."

"Not just now actually," Boris said and walked past his father back into the dining room.

ANDREA turned round briefly to look at her brother. Boris was asleep in the back seat, snoring, his head on Poison's shoulder.

She swivelled her head to look at Leo again.

"What did you think of Roz?"

"Quite nice. And your dad seemed ... more relaxed; more cheerful than he usually is."

"You've only seen him before when Desmond's been about.

That's probably why. And there's the new girlfriend factor."

"I suppose so."

"You obviously liked her. But ... Do you think she's just using Dad?"

"What do you mean?"

"Well, it was just that she seemed very interested in Boris. She was sort of grilling us before he turned up and then…"

Andrea turned to face the rear again for a few seconds. Boris was still asleep. Poison was staring out of the window, apparently disinterested.

"…she kept looking at him. And me. I just felt she had some sort of angle. I mean Boris knows that DC of hers. It seems a sort of circular thing. And it was her who wanted this dinner together tonight."

"I can't imagine what exactly she might be using him for. Most likely she's just interested in her new boyfriend's family. Why wouldn't she be?"

Andrea heaved a sigh. "Maybe. But I reckon Dad's besotted with her. I'd hate to see him get hurt."

"He's a big grown up lawyer, Andrea. I shouldn't worry about him too much. And we're at Boris's house now."

Leo tilted his head to the left once the car was stationary.

"Er, Poison, do you want us to take you somewhere or will you get out with Boris? And can you wake him up."

"'S OK. You can drop us both here."

Poison shook Boris awake. They practically fell out of the car. Poison slammed the door and they walk in a disorderly fashion towards the house.

Leo watched them, laughing. Andrea looked at him and then away at Boris and Poison, her face the picture of worry.

"IT was clever of Stefka to have thought of bringing in distilled water for the steam iron," said Guy later in bed, "even though that girl wouldn't drink it." Poison had said that the water should be freshly distilled or else it would have absorbed contamination from the air.

Roz was laughing, as she had been in fact since Boris and

Poison had left with Leo and Andrea soon after their chat. Andrea was used to Boris's ways but still hadn't seemed much amused. Unlike Leo. At least Roz wasn't offended.

"Come on. You have to see the funny side."

"Do I?" said Guy. He was also put out that Roz had told him as they came up the stairs that there was a barbecue birthday party the following afternoon. They'd agreed on a weekend of almost total carnal activity yet now she wanted them to go to this do.

But Roz was working her magic on him and, turning to her, he soon forgot his grouches.

Chapter 12

"IT won't be *all* coppers at this thing will it?" said Guy, as they drove along the road to the house.

"Well, there'll be wives and girlfriends too."

"I qualify as a girlfriend, do I?"

"You know what I mean. Other halves."

The birthday boy, Len, was the fifty-five year old Detective Chief Inspector Guy had seen on TV with Roz last week. He was standing next to the barbecue in the rear garden knocking back lager and laughing with some other men.

Guy had taken Roz's hand after they got out of the car, however she'd disengaged once they were past the side of the house. The tough career woman with no visible weaknesses was obviously back.

Roz led Guy over to say hello to Len and introduce him.

"Glad you could make it," said Len. "Help yourselves to some burgers and booze. The booze is over there."

He gestured to a table barely visible behind a crowd.

"If you can get near it."

"Oh. Mustn't forget your prezz," said Roz, and handed over a gift wrapped parcel. It looked like a book and he thanked her, putting it on a side table with other unopened presents.

So, Guy thought, she must've known about this party before yesterday.

"Cheers, Roz. Perhaps we can have a quick word a bit later."

"Course."

Guy had been quiet throughout, his face expressionless.

"Happy birthday, Len," he said. "Speak to you later I hope."

Roz took Guy over to the table with the plates, salads, sauces and so on. There were loads of people here, groups of women talking, whether partners or officers Guy didn't know, children running about, table tennis and a few other little games going on. Guy as usual was famished and started to heap up his plate.

"I'll go and get us some meat," said Roz. "Can you serve me a little bit of green salad and some potato salad."

And she walked off. To the barbecue. And didn't come back.

Guy watched Len and Roz stroll away from the press of people round the barbecue and they disappeared into the house.

"Bugger," he said to himself. He took a slice of cold quiche and went and sat down at a large table where there was a spare seat.

He cast his eyes every so often towards the conservatory by which Roz and Len had entered the house.

"She's deserted you then," said one man. "Too bad, mate. Have a beer."

"Thanks," said Guy, accepting the bottle.

"You known Roz long then?" another man asked.

"Well, for many years I suppose."

The table waited for an explanation. Guy thought he'd better be as discreet as possible.

"In a past life, I worked as a criminal solicitor around here. About twenty-five, thirty odd years ago. Possibly before your time. So I knew her then. Not well though."

Guy glanced towards the conservatory. A young woman sitting next to him who said she was a DS, told Guy that Roz'd be back soon.

"Don't worry. It's police all over to come to a party and then talk shop. And we've got a number of tricky cases on at the moment. I'm Pam by the way."

"Hello. I'm Guy. Pleased to meet you."

The rest of the table got back to their previous conversations.

"So, is it all CID here then? No uniformed or clerical staff?"

"Pretty much. What do you do now?"

"I lecture at a university on contract and tort. Though my pet enthusiasm is jurisprudence. The law courses barely touch on it so it's mostly a hobby."

Pam obviously hadn't got a clue what he was talking about.

"Right. Jurisprudence is an academic subject. Er, it includes various theories, for example what morality has to do with the law. The history of the law. How it's developed, and indeed is likely to develop."

Pam looked blank and Guy laughed.

"Yes, well, it's ... not something you'd come across very often."

Pam nodded and Guy sipped his beer. He smiled at Pam whose eyes had begun to glaze over.

"Oh," he said. "Here comes Roz. It was nice meeting you. If you'll excuse me..."

He stood and, seeing Roz approaching on her own bearing some burgers and sausages on a paper plate, he walked over to her balancing their two plates of salad and his beer. He followed her to a small empty table.

"This is more like it," he speared a sausage, in a better mood now.

"Sorry about that. Just a few developments."

"About what?"

"Just cases."

"The murder of the Romanian girl?"

"Well, yes, as you ask."

"So what's new?"

Roz lowered her voice. "Guy, you know I shouldn't be talking to you in any detail about cases."

"Don't you trust me?"

Roz looked up from her plate. Guy's eyes had turned rather flinty, rather cold. It surprised her since he was usually so laid back and easy-going.

"Who's grilling whom now! It's not a question of not trusting. It's my duty not to disclose details of cases. If you were still a practising solicitor, would you tell me all sorts of things about specific cases?"

"Probably, yes. If you were interested."

"Well it's not the same. The girl's name's been in the newspapers. We've had a televised appeal for information for heaven's sake. If you told me about cases you were dealing with, unless they were incredibly high profile, the clients would still be anonymous."

Guy looked away and sank his beer. They'd been talking in low voices. He glanced across the lawn and saw birthday boy peering at them over his own glass. Roz noticed too.

"Look," she said, "let's have another drink. Then perhaps after that we can go for a little walk." She pointed to some bushes. "Through that shrubbery there's a gate onto a public footpath at the back."

"How d'you know that?"

"I've been here before, of course."

"Not one of your 'odd romances' was he?"

Roz sighed. "Maybe," she said.

"All right then." Guy gave a crooked smile. "And perhaps you'll let me hold your hand if we're alone."

Chapter 13

THE footpath was rather overgrown and, Roz would hazard, little used in spite of the fact that all these houses backed onto it. It was quiet, with a rural air, and you'd never know you were in the heart of the commuter-belt, just a stone's throw from a station directly to Kings Cross.

They were walking along slowly, more relaxed now that they were away from her colleagues. Guy put his arm around Roz and nuzzled her hair.

"I do trust you," she said.

"'S all right. I was being unreasonable."

"It isn't much anyway," Roz said. "It's just that we've been in touch with the girl's family in Romania, and they're a lot better off than would be normal. It's still a poor country by our standards."

"So?"

"Well, someone's been giving them large chunks of cash as far as we can make out. But there's no paper trail, no electronic trail and the family aren't saying anything. And there's no sign of the brother in England."

They walked in silence for a time, both pensive.

Finally, Roz took a deep breath and continued.

"It'd be handy to get the males of the family DNA tested in Romania but we can't do that, at least without more evidence. The man of Hispanic extraction whose DNA we found could come from anywhere. We can't get every country where there's a Hispanic/Latino population to open their records to us. We think the murder's either some sort of family thing or a contract killing.

Guy looked keenly at Roz. "You mean she was blackmailing someone and they got her bumped off?"

"Yes, basically," said Roz, determinedly studying the ground. "Quite what any blackmail might have been about is anyone's guess at the moment. She was secretive when she was alive. If she'd told us more about the threats she said she was getting, we might have been able to do something to help her, perhaps prevent what happened to her."

Guy nodded. "Yes. Pity I suppose."

Roz tried not to scrutinize Guy too closely while they discussed these things. She didn't want a repetition of last Sunday when her heart had stopped beating over the possibility that he might be about to dump her. She had to look down anyway to avoid standing on any dog poo. It looked like dog walkers, at least, used this poorly maintained path.

"What we need is someone to come forward with information," she said. "Whoever visited the deceased was very careful not to be seen. No one in the building she lived in or roundabouts saw anything apparently."

"No CCTV evidence?"

"None. No cameras at all in the vicinity."

"Oh. I thought they were everywhere."

"No. Not even doorbell cameras. They're becoming more popular."

"What about the officer who found her though?" Guy asked. "You seem to have discounted him. But isn't it the case that the person who finds the body sometimes turns out to be the perpetrator?"

"Don't think we haven't considered that possibility. But the girl was strangled. Mal's hands don't match the bruising to her neck. The man who did it had much bigger hands."

Roz thought about this.

"And Mal's actually not remotely the type to be a killer."

"Is that the friend of Boris? Mal. Short for?"

"Yes. Malcolm, I think."

They walked on in silence again.

Roz was mulling over how strange it was that Andrea and Boris were so unalike. Both fair-haired and blue-eyed for sure, yet that's as far as it went. Their features were plainly totally different. She hadn't seen the ex-wife Liz, but neither of them looked like Guy who was dark. However she didn't say anything and–

"How long do we have to stay here?" asked Guy.

"Well, there's fireworks planned for later."

"What! It won't be dark for at least another four hours."

"Don't worry. I told him we had to leave at five-thirty so you could go to a family do."

"Roz, you're an angel." He kissed her.

"We'd better go back," she said.

GUY hadn't had this dream for many years.

"We didn't do anything. We didn't do anything wrong. It didn't happen that way," he was trying to say. No matter how he strained, the words wouldn't come out.

He heaved and writhed and groaned until all his systems forced his sleep-paralysed body to erupt into wakefulness and his mind to start to function in the real world.

"Didn't," he shouted.

And his brain registered the horrifying fact that he was lying next to a member of the constabulary. His worst night-time fear was apprehension by the police though, instead of handcuffing him, the officer climbed on top of him and kissed him full on the lips. Unexpected. All the same, still half in never-never-land, he responded in kind.

"I love you, Roz," he told her softly.

And all the dire possibilities faded away.

"YOU had a bad dream last night."

"Hmm. Did I say anything?"

"Not really. You just yelled something like 'Don't', that's all."

"Well, you dealt with it very effectively."

They were in bed Sunday morning, Guy having trotted downstairs and made and brought up a cup of tea each for them. Roz had, however, wrapped herself around him so he couldn't actually drink any of his. Never mind.

"Guy, darling." *Darling.*

"Hmm."

"You told me you loved me last night. Did you mean it?"

He raised himself up a little and looked down into her eyes.

He was silent for a moment.

"Yes," he said. "Do you love me?"

"Yes."

"Tell me then."

"I love you, Guy."

This was it. Their moment of no-going-back. As they looked deep into each other's eyes, their souls mingled and held firm, something of each planted and rooted unshakeably within the other. That part so transplanted would remain in the other forever, regardless of the physical constraints of time and space, forming an unbreakable thread between them. So is the feeling of true lovers. They may each have and hold their secrets, but nothing could touch the essential bond formed in those minutes.

They sealed the bond with a soft and tender kiss. Then they drew apart, smiling a little shyly to each other, and took their tea, both thinking their thoughts.

BACK in Lincoln again, Guy sat down in his small crowded office at the University. For many years he had combed auction rooms, second-hand bookshops and libraries and attended sales which included the assets of legal firms who had either gone bust or merged, looking for redundant works which might render useful historical information for his passion, jurisprudence. He similarly checked the 'for sale' sections of the Law Society Gazette and other publications and, of course, all the online auction and other similar sites.

His small office here at the university had proved unequal to the growing library, so that rooms at home and the garage had had to be appropriated, proving a considerable bone of contention with the former second Mrs Attwood.

Would Roz have put up with it? A question unlikely to be tested. Since the divorce and his enforced house move, a summerhouse in the garden of his present home accommodated his books so the house itself was less cluttered than it might have been.

He ruminated absently when Roz might come and visit him

instead of his travelling to Hertfordshire on the weekends.

Now, though, he had a singular task to perform. Following the mention of blackmail and a contract killing, Guy had speculated about Paul, the East End thug who drove Liz and Desmond about and fixed things for them, though so far as Guy knew, as he'd said to Andrea, it was things like plumbing contractors, domestic cleaners, dog kennels, holidays, et cetera.

It was ages since he'd called Liz. There was no need once parental contact arrangements had ceased to be necessary years ago. He hoped she had the same mobile number. He needed to arrange to meet her. Soon. He knew what she'd expect him to do about his relationship with Roz, but she'd have to accept that that was off the agenda.

It was likely that at this time of day, lunchtime, she'd be home alone with no Desmond to listen in. He looked up her number and pressed to call her.

Chapter 14

THE incident room was buzzing. It was Thursday the following week and Len had called a brainstorming meeting in the about the Romanian girl. Everyone involved in the case had to attend unless they were out on an emergency.

The information on the white board was expanding. Amongst other things, there were photos of the girl alive and dead. There were a number of columns with some cross-referencing. Two were headed up with respectively 'Unknown Romanian Brother' and 'Unknown Hispanic Man'. A third column had a new entry Roz hadn't seen before: 'Unknown Englishman'. It made her feel distinctly uneasy.

There were theories on the board such as the perpetrator having been interrupted, that it was a family killing, that it was a contract killing.

There was also a section for other theories, good ideas but weak ones for which there was no evidence, for example a thwarted boyfriend, a burglary gone wrong, a random attack, the wrong house and therefore a mistake.

"Right," said Len at the head of the room. "Quiet please. Let's get on with it.

"OK, given the cash we think was being paid to the Romanian family, our favourite theory, as you know, is that the girl was blackmailing someone and they had her murdered by a contract killer. The reason we don't think the person immediately being blackmailed was the murderer is that the individual who organised it obviously had enough money to enable cash to be paid to the family, leaving no records whatever and no trail back to himself, or indeed herself, which suggests a well-off person with maybe some underworld or gangland connection. The person responsible wasn't going to sully their hands strangling a girl or running off to Romania with sacks of cash. This took organisation. It could have been a woman just as well as a man.

"On the other hand, we haven't found a scrap of mobile or

internet traffic from or to Ileana that might suggest she was blackmailing someone or who it was. If she *was* blackmailing someone, then she was just as good as they were at keeping it below the radar. Olly's been right through Ileana's laptop, smart phone and work PC and there's not a trace of anything suggestive blackmail or anything untoward. She was receiving email threats as well as in other forms, but there's nothing about blackmail. Just innocent contact with her family back in Romania. So maybe there was no blackmail and the brother was the murderer.

"But if so, why would he murder his sister? Sibling rivalry? Jealousy? And who was this man? There's no record of any man in the family coming to England to work as Ileana did.

"If she *was* blackmailing someone, then surely the threats she reported were to do with that. Trying to frighten her into stopping the blackmail. But reporting the threats to us seems a bit of a risky thing for her to have done. If we'd actually found anything out, it might have uncovered the blackmail too.

"Anyone have any theories about that?" Len finished.

A young male DS spoke up. "Yes, but although she reported the threats, she wasn't very co-operative about it. Perhaps her real intention was to send a message to the person she was blackmailing that she had guts and wasn't going to be frightened off. Of course, that could have sealed her fate with the blackmailer deciding they had to do away with her, or at least frighten her really badly; like having her seriously beaten up, say."

"It certainly could have," said Len. "Very good point." Len jotted a note on the board.

"OK. We don't expect to find out any more about the Hispanic man. If he was a contract killer, he'll be long gone. It's assumed he watched the building and knew the routines of the other flat occupiers and therefore when the building would be empty, apart from the girl.

"As to who interrupted the murder, perhaps that was the Romanian brother, if he wasn't actually himself the murderer. Perhaps the brother had had regular contact with the girl and just happened to go there that evening. If so, he was lucky not to have been killed himself by the murderer. A contract killer can be expected to be totally cold-blooded, prepared to remove anyone who got in his way. Perhaps the killer hid in the flat and got out without having to do anything to the brother."

A DS spoke up. Pamela Chambers:

"Perhaps the killer had instructions not to hurt the brother."

"Good point," said Len writing it on the board with the word 'Why' and a question mark.

"Maybe," said Pamela, "there was some sort of family situation here in the UK, as well as in Romania."

"Good," said Len and wrote that on the board with a question mark. "Come on. Let's have more ideas. We don't just want my ideas."

"Perhaps the brother got a look at the killer as the killer fled," said DC Olly Barlow. "Odd, then, that he hasn't come forward with information if his sister had just been killed. In that case, he may know who the organiser of the murder was and is either frightened of him/her or the person is close to him and he isn't prepared to do anything to give them away." The board was filling up.

Pamela said "Possibly the killer only intended to frighten her. But he got interrupted too quickly to do very much, panicked, and killed her."

"Very possible," said Len, noting this down.

Another officer asked: "This brother. Isn't there any record of him in Romania? Birth records, et cetera?"

"Well," said Len, "those of you who're old enough will recall that twenty, twenty-five-odd years ago there was an influx of Romanian orphans into this country. Romania was a desperately poor country, a Catholic country. No contraception. Huge families. Girls, women would leave their babies in orphanages where the conditions were appalling. Record-keeping wasn't likely to have been a priority. Bordering Serbia was in conflict with its neighbour. There must have been some turmoil."

"But why," asked a DS, "are we assuming twenty-five years

ago? Why a brother in his mid-twenties? We've been told the Romanian family have children ranging up to forty years old now."

"Good point," said Len. "Which brings me on to this, and the possible reason for the blackmailing." He aimed his pointer at the words 'Unknown Englishman'.

Roz swallowed and looked down at her empty jotter.

"An older brother has broken cover and given some unexpected information which I've just received. He says that about twenty-three years ago, an Englishman drove by their then home and bought the youngest little boy in the family who was a year old at that time. He handed over cash. The man went off with the boy and they never saw him again. The boy was called..." Len consulted his notes, "...er, Matei. Like Matthew in English, I understand."

He paused for effect. "And he had a twin sister. Ileana Bratianu."

There were gasps around the room.

"Yes," said Len. "Quite a story."

Roz felt her face grow hot and sweat break out all over her body. She thought she was over hot flushes but this felt just like one, including the nausea.

Len continued. "Might this Englishman be the mastermind behind the murder? The brother who disclosed this is now so frightened that he's gone into hiding. We hope he'll keep in touch through one of our intermediaries."

Another officer piped up. "Is it reliable though? If he was paid, could he be trusted to tell the truth?"

"He was paid, yes, but otherwise we wouldn't have got anything. We must hope that he or someone else in the family provides information that enables us to identify the Englishman. I think he's the key to this case. OK, I'll have to wrap the meeting up. Any more ideas? Roz?" Len said suddenly. "You've been very quiet. Any thoughts? Surely you must have a few ideas."

"Not that I can think of," said Roz, outwardly calm.

"It must be affecting your concentration. Getting too much

attention from that new boyfriend of yours?" another DI said. He wasn't working directly on the case. Too many DIs spoiled the broth. But he was required to keep abreast of developments. There was general laughter. There was only one way to treat such a comment.

"Not getting enough attention yourself in that department? *You're* just jealous," she smiled.

"Come on. Break it up," said Len. You never knew where these jibes might lead. He didn't want it degenerating into a situation that might result in a complaint. He wished now that he hadn't thrown the spotlight on Roz. "OK. We'll call it a day." He named a few officers to go to his room for some follow-up jobs.

Roz glanced at the photos of the girl before going back to her desk as quickly as possible to tidy it and close down her PC, glad that she had the rest of the afternoon off. She'd been in since six and she wanted some time to rest and think. She saw the officer's troop out of Len's room and she started to make for the door.

"Could I see you for a moment, Roz."

It was Len. She could hardly refuse.

"Sure," she said and followed him to his room. Out of the corner of her eye, she saw others watching. She ignored them and closed the door, aware though that she and Len could be seen inside the glass partitioned office.

Len invited her to sit down.

"Thanks for the book by the way. I haven't had a chance to thank you since Sunday."

"Actually I won't sit, Len. I'm due the afternoon off and I'm quite tired. I'm looking forward to having a rest."

"It's a shame we didn't get more of a chance to talk on Sunday. I barely spoke to ... Guy wasn't it? Something of an intellectual so I'm told. And he used to work around here. As a criminal solicitor."

Aware that Len was scrutinising her, she answered shortly.

"Yes."

She wasn't alarmed. Len often used this trick on his team,

hoping to wheedle out something extra. He probably noticed she was particularly tired and grumpy and thought she might tell him why.

"I don't remember him. It must've been before I came here."

"Yes. I expect so." She tried for a light-hearted note. "As you know, I've been here since practically leaving kindergarten. But Len, I'd quite like to be making tracks if you don't mind. It's been a hard few weeks."

"OK. Sure. But, if anything's worrying you, you know you can talk to me. Any time."

"Course. Thanks. I'm fine. Just tired."

"Yeah. I understand."

There was a pause as Len continued to stare, though kindly enough.

"I just thought in there."

Was he going to question her failure to contribute? Apparently not.

"I don't know why we haven't done it before. The brother who told us about the purchase of a child could well have been lying. I'll get a couple of the others onto researching the adoptions from Romania. I s'pose we assumed the brother had somehow got to England recently. But he might be an adoptee from years ago."

Roz was silent.

"Good idea or what?

Sighing, Roz replied: "Well, it's something."

"All right. I can see you're done in. Off you go. Bye, Roz. See you tomorrow."

"Yeah. See you."

She walked out. Len watched her go, thoughtful.

Chapter 15

GUY was not in Hertfordshire and he wasn't in Lincoln. He'd been asked to guest lecture on jurisprudence for a few days at Oxford University. As a result, he had told Roz that he wasn't able to see her during the forthcoming weekend. This wasn't strictly true, but all the same, it wouldn't hurt to not see Roz for just the one weekend. Although actually it *was* hurting.

He had spoken to Liz and had arranged to meet her. He'd hoped it would be this week some time, but she'd claimed to be far too busy. He'd found Liz's attitude strange in the circumstances, given that he bore no responsibility for the recent developments. She was cold, distant and evasive.

He'd been forced to accept an appointment with her next Wednesday. Well, it had felt like arranging an appointment with someone's officious diary secretary. He had imagined that they could chat amicably and collude as necessary to try to avert any problems for the family but she stonewalled him on the phone. He'd had to agree to the meeting being at a service area café on the A1. She'd insisted.

Many years of being a rich woman able to command more or less anything she wanted seemed to have changed her and made her selfish and self-centred. Perhaps it would be better when they were face-to-face.

Roz hadn't said much when he cried off the weekend and he couldn't tell if she was upset or not. Now though, he found he was unable to concentrate on preparing for tomorrow's lecture and he knew that if it went on much longer, he'd have to call Roz and see if she would still be able to meet this weekend.

WITHOUT meaning to, Roz had fallen asleep on the settee with the TV on and she woke with a start when the doorbell rang. It was just gone five pm. She hurried to the door.

She was surprised to see that it was Boris, clutching flowers and a box of chocolates which he held out. She stared at his big hands as he passed them over to her.

"Peace offering. To say sorry," he said. They stood there for some seconds until Roz collected herself and invited him in.

"There was no need. Would you like a cup of tea or coffee?"

"Well..."

"Oh. I suppose for you city slickers it's wine-bar time now. I'll dig a bottle out of the fridge and join you. Sit down."

She was back soon with the bottle and glasses. "Not at work today?"

"Hmm this is nice," he said taking a sip. "No. I took a few days off. Actually I've carried on seeing Poison and she works some evenings in a bar so I've spent a couple of days with her."

Roz laughed. "Doesn't she have a proper name?"

"Probably," he said vaguely.

Roz decided he was rather charming in his evasive way. With his mop of blond hair, he looked a bit like Boris Johnson, but vastly better-looking and, though big, not fat. And of course he was terribly posh like Andrea.

"Well that's nice anyway. That you're still seeing her. Though taking her out for a meal or even a drink must be a bit of a challenge."

"Hmm. We haven't done much eating or drinking actually, so it hasn't been a problem."

"Oh. Well. Good."

She wondered what they would talk about for the next half hour or so. She assumed he wouldn't be staying much longer than that.

"You seeing Dad this weekend?"

"No," she sighed. "You know he's at Oxford this week and part of next week. He said he was guest lecturing on his pet subject. Juris ... thingummyjig. Apparently he couldn't spare the time."

"No, I didn't know. About Oxford. Oh well, perhaps you'll work this weekend. Isn't that what you police officers do? My mate Mal is always having to work odd hours. He found that Romanian girl didn't he?"

"I suppose he must have told you that. Yes, he did." Roz

looked away. "I'll go and get a snack," she said and got up. However he followed her into the kitchen and stood hovering near her as she poked about in a cupboard.

"Are you any nearer to finding the killer?" Boris asked.

"Boris, obviously I can't discuss it. We're doing our best."

"You must have some idea though."

"We're working on it. That's all I can say."

He looked at her coldly. He was just a foot or so away and she started to feel threatened. As she straightened up with a packet of Bombay Mix in her hand, she was face-to-face with him, trapped by the cupboard door. Neither of them said anything. He was so big. For a second she pictured the face of Ileana Bratianu staring seriously out from the photos of her when she was still alive, superimposed on the features of Boris before her. She felt sure he knew she was frightened of him. She shook her head trying to find something to say. Something normal and ordinary.

"I'll get a vase," she said. "For the flowers." She tried to edge past him but he didn't move.

"Is there any new evidence?" Boris was watching her intently and he moved fractionally closer.

What evidence, Roz thought, could he possibly know about already, conscious that she might be alone in the presence of a murderer. Someone who had strangled a girl with his bare hands, though how he might have known Ileana or why he would have killed her, Roz feared to acknowledge.

But Boris suddenly turned away.

"I'd better go," he said.

"Oh really. So soon?"

Boris gave a mirthless half-laugh to himself. "Give my love to Dad if you talk to him," he said. She caught sarcasm in his tone. He walked out.

Roz sighed with relief. She immediately walked around the house, bolting the doors and checking the windows. She wondered if she'd imagined Boris having apparently tried to scare her. Because that was what it had felt like. His attitude had seemed predatory, threatening. She had sensed that he'd really intended to frighten her. Was he trying to force her to tell him something? Or warn her? If so, about what? And to what end?

BY the time Guy phoned her, Roz had had a few glasses of wine on her own.

"Roz," said Guy. "I think, actually, if you're still free this weekend, I should be able to make it down there."

"Oh. OK."

"You don't sound very pleased."

"Of course I am. It's just that I'm feeling a bit odd. We ... well ... we had a session at the station today about, you know, the *case*, and then Boris came round here and–"

"Boris? What for?"

She told him about the apology and the gifts.

"Oh. Good," said Guy, surprised.

"I suppose so."

"Roz, are you OK? You don't sound your usual self."

"Yes. I expect it was just the case and having a strange man alone in the house with me. I don't know. It felt..."

"Felt what?"

"Well. Just a bit scary, that's all."

"Roz, this is Boris we're talking about. My son. What did he say to make you scared? He didn't do anything did he?"

"Hmm, well ... no, nothing specific."

"Roz, can I come down tomorrow evening? I need to see you anyway."

"Why? Is there something you want to tell me?"

"No. Of course not. I just want to see you. You know? Us? You and me? What we said last weekend?"

"Oh. Yes, right."

"Roz, you do love me don't you? I love you."

"Yes, Guy, you know I do. I wish you were here now."

"I wish I was there too. Pity you can't come up here and spend the weekend. They've given me a college room. It looks out over a quadrangle. The atmosphere's stunning. It makes you think of toasting crumpets. Although of course there's no fire in the grate just now. You deserve a break."

"Gosh, that would be nice. I'd jump in the car immediately but I've had a few glasses of wine."

"Could you get the time off?"

"Probably."

"Come by train."

"I'll find out and text you."

"Great. That's great. See you later then, hopefully."

They hung up. So much, thought Guy, for his powers of determination. He obviously had the resolve of a bowl of lukewarm semolina. He started to look forward to the visit very much. That thing about Boris was a bit worrying though.

Chapter 16

IN A packed lecture room at Oxford University, Guy stood at a lectern. It was Friday and he hadn't seen Roz all day apart from kissing her goodbye after quickly showering and dressing this morning. Yesterday, by the time she'd arrived it was late, they were both tired and had tumbled into bed.

Guy intended to give his full attention to Roz over the weekend. He'd largely already prepared in advance for his lectures and should be able to keep the weekend free for leisure and pleasure. He was looking forward to it. He did hope Roz would perk up though. She'd been distant and uncommunicative yesterday evening and he couldn't understand why.

"Of course," he addressed his audience, "you will all know that murder has been regarded for centuries as a fundamental wrong, you might say a moral wrong, part of natural law, so heinous as to previously be punishable by death in this country. Even today, the crime is a common law crime; contrary to common law, not statute. Which is, if you think about it, surprising."

He paused to sip water from a glass on a small table by his side. He looked up as a door at the back of the room opened a crack, then further. A figure squeezed partway through, as though trying not to attract attention. He smiled, seeing Roz half in and half out of the room but she didn't respond. Instead, she ducked out and shut the door.

Guy sighed unhappily.

"Nonetheless," he told the room, "this didn't prevent earlier societies from condoning horrific acts such as lynchings, based on moral judgements and mob mentality which we would today regard as wholly unacceptable, regardless of our own points of view on the conduct of the victim.

"This week, we've concentrated on the history of law in general. Next week, we will move on to the concept of ownership from ancient times up to the present day, including something called blockchain technology and similar ideas which could alter the way property changes hands. We'll consider how modern society deals with ownership rights as well as the acquisition and transfer process. I'm using the word 'property', incidentally, in the wider sense of anything that can be owned, not just houses, factories, land, and so on."

With that, he took some questions, then wrapped up the afternoon, anxious to meet up with Roz and have dinner.

ROZ was seated at a small table by the time Guy arrived at the Eagle & Child. The place was packed, the tourist season in full swing. He kissed Roz and sat down, trying to appear cheerful, hearty, though it was slightly forced and he knew Roz wouldn't be deceived.

"I don't blame you for not staying to hear the end of the lecture. Although, actually, that lot seemed to like it quite a lot."

Roz's watery smile didn't reach her eyes.

"I decided not to disturb your flow."

"So, what have you been up to all day?

"Just wandering around. I went into the Ashmolean. You could spend several weeks in there, there's so much to see."

"Shall we order? I've already decided on steak and ale pie."

"Oh. I don't mind what I have. I'm not very hungry."

"Did you go somewhere for lunch then?"

"Er, no. But ... you know me."

Guy bit his lip.

"Yes. But you're obviously upset about something. Last night ... well you weren't your usual self shall we say."

"I'm just tired, Guy."

He took her hand.

"Are you sure that's all it is? I can't think how Boris could have frightened you yesterday. He's just ... such a big softie."

"I didn't actually say he frightened me. Or not deliberately. I don't suppose. I expect I'm just tense from ... everything."

Guy nodded. If there was a real problem, he didn't feel like acknowledging it and bringing it into the open this weekend.

Better to play along with the tiredness excuse.

"Yes, well. Anyway, we've been invited to a cocktail party tomorrow night. Would you like that?"

Roz looked alarmed, then wilted.

"Oh." Her shoulders slumped.

Guy cast his eyes up and down Roz's face, concerned; in fact, slightly exasperated.

"I thought it would be an experience for both of us. A treat. Simeon's parties are supposed to be legendary. But of course we don't have to go if you don't want to."

"You go. I'll ... watch TV or read."

"No way. I want to spend the time with you. It's no big deal. I can easily get out of it."

Roz sniffed, eyes watering.

"Roz, darling. Please tell me what's wrong." He hoped this wouldn't produce anything catastrophic, at least for their relationship, but he couldn't help asking. "Look we're not staying here if you feel so awful."

Guy took his hand away and produced a handkerchief. He received no clear answer.

"It's not fair on you," Roz told him. "I shouldn't have come."

"I don't mind. As long as I'm with you, it doesn't matter to me that you're under the weather. If it's something else, I hope you'd tell me."

"But you're famished. You always are."

Her face softened and she smiled.

"That's a bit better. We'll get a takeaway. And tomorrow night too."

"I think I'd better get the train back Sunday evening. Or earlier. Rather than Monday morning. We're so busy at work and I need a good night's sleep on Sunday. You don't mind too much do you?"

Guy's face fell.

"Well, that's a shame. I hoped it'd be a treat for you to be here."

Roz turned away, her expression closed. Guy peered at her,

trying not to upset things any further by showing how worried he was.

ROZ sat in the railway carriage, absently scanning the passing countryside. It was a roundabout journey between Oxford and Hatford, getting off at Paddington, taking the tube to Kings Cross St Pancras and then northwards out of London to Hatford. She wished she'd been able to drive to Oxford on Thursday evening and then it would have been so much quicker to have driven back today, Saturday.

She'd found she couldn't stomach nearly two more days with Guy until Monday morning, her intended departure time. He'd tried of course to dissuade her from leaving so soon. He hadn't understood, so it appeared, though she suspected that was a façade and he was hiding his real feelings.

Then he had wanted to drive her back to Hatford and spend the rest of the weekend with her. She'd had to be firmer than she would have wished to deflect his urgent demands. She'd refused to even let him drive her to the station to catch this early train, calling a taxi while he was in the bathroom.

Her actual leave-taking had been quiet, she buttoning-up her inner grief, he tight-lipped and resentful. There'd be time for tears later, no doubt in bucketsful in her case.

At the moment she needed to think. Think about her past and what she could recall of Guy's time in Hatford, what firm he'd worked for, whether she might be able to speak to anyone from the firm who would have known him during that period.

Heaven knew, enough of her thoughts had centred around him those years ago when they were in their twenties. It had threatened to become an obsession. She'd sometimes had to stop herself from calling him, making some sort of proposition to him. Only the shame of the anticipated rejection held her back. She hadn't wanted to become a sad case.

She'd forced all this, him, to the back of her mind for over two decades in order to get on with her career and lead a stable life, make friends, get married – then divorced, of course.

All these things had filled the time until that Saturday just four weeks ago, when her eyes had once again locked with his and she'd been unable to break the contact, leaving him to do so. The joy when his daughter had brought him over to speak to her had been almost irrepressible, a physical surge of both ecstasy and hope. She'd had to mask it then and since with a veneer of unconcern. It wasn't at all easy.

Blake & Munnings. That was the name of the firm of solicitors she'd tried so hard not to telephone and ask to speak to their assistant solicitor, Guy Attwood. Her face grew hot even now at the thought of making such a call, having such an imagined conversation with Guy.

She already had her laptop open on the empty seat beside her. She could have used her smart phone, but preferred the laptop on which she could better save any documents or pages she found.

She knew Blake & Munnings didn't exist any longer but nonetheless she Googled the name. It was one of those older firms that kept the same name even if partners changed. She wasn't aware that there had ever been a partner called Blake as long as she'd worked in Hatford, but she vaguely remembered a Mr Munnings. The Google search came up straightaway with another firm which turned out to be a successor firm. In twenty years, there'd been a lot of mergers and takeovers of legal firms.

It took her the rest of the journey to Paddington to find out that Derek Munnings was no longer a partner, having retired, that he had previously served as a District Councillor and had held other public positions and that he'd been a director of several companies. It wasn't difficult from these sources to find his home address.

Chapter 17

ROZ slammed her car door and walked slowly along the suburban street of older expensive properties, checking her note and staring at the house numbers. She stopped outside a house with a 'For Sale/Sold' sign in the front garden. She hoped she wasn't too late and would find that the Munnings had moved. It was two pm, just after lunch, so any occupiers would be more likely to be at home.

She wasn't sure quite what she expected to discover. It felt like snooping; snooping on Guy's past. She was uncomfortable about it, but she couldn't do nothing. Her instincts more than anything else told her there was something going on. The suspicions which had been slowly crystallising since Thursday seemed fantastic and if her enquiries came to nothing, then it would be a huge relief.

But she wasn't one to avoid facing up to the truth whatever that may be and this exercise would at least keep her occupied for the time being. Composing herself, she walked to the front door, rang the bell and waited.

A woman in her seventies answered the door.

"Hello?" the woman said.

Roz flashed her warrant card. She'd taken it to Oxford with her. In fact, she always kept it on her.

"I'm sorry to bother you. I believe you're Mrs Munnings. My name's Detective Inspector Roz Benedict. I'm investigating the murder of a Romanian girl several weeks ago. You've probably heard about it. It's been on the news."

"Oh yes?"

"We're just trying to eliminate one or two things. I wondered if I could have a word with you."

A puzzled expression crossed Mrs Munnings's face.

"I'm afraid I don't see how I could help. I know almost nothing about it. I haven't even been listening to the news reports much. As you can see, the house is sold and I've had a lot to do. My husband died earlier this year and it's too big for me."

The death of Mr Munnings hadn't come up during Roz's internet investigations.

"I'm so sorry about that. I hadn't realised. It was your late husband I really wanted to ask."

"Derek? I can't see what it could have had to do with him."

Mrs Munnings didn't say this unpleasantly but she was starting to be dismissive in a matter-of-fact sort of way.

"No," Roz said quickly. "It's someone who worked for him I wanted to speak to you about. As I say, it's just for elimination."

A woman walked by. She looked curiously at Roz and waved at Mrs Munnings, slowing down, craning her neck. Mrs Munnings waved back.

She sighed. "You'd better come in."

"Yes, thanks very much."

She followed Mrs Munnings into the house and into a sitting room off the hall. Packing cases were everywhere.

"Take a seat," said Mrs Mummings. "Sorry it's such a mess but I'm moving next week. I'll get some tea. I've just boiled the kettle as it happens. Or would you prefer coffee?"

"That'd be very kind. Coffee please."

The older woman bustled off. Roz waited, looking about, then removed a notebook and pen from her bag, another accoutrement of her police life that went everywhere with her.

Very soon, Mrs Munnings walked in with a tray.

"Help yourself to milk and sugar or whatever. Right you'd better tell me what you want to know. But Derek retired six years ago. Poor soul, he had almost no retirement. I wouldn't know anything about the employees at the firm after that."

"I'm sorry to hear that," Roz repeated, and carried on outlining things while she added milk to her cup. "It wasn't actually his last firm that I was going to ask you about. I understand the firm had several amalgamations over the years. The period I'm interested in is twenty to twenty-five years ago when I think it was just a small firm with three partners and Mr Munnings was one of them."

"You mean when they were called Blake & Munnings?"

"Yes, that would have been it. I'll try and keep it brief. Can you remember that a solicitor called Guy Attwood worked there? He was a criminal lawyer. He–"

"Of course I remember Guy. I worked there myself some of the time doing secretarial work. I was quite involved at that time. Our sons were away at school and I wanted something to do."

To the police detective in Roz, this was just the sort of thing she was hoping to hear.

"Oh, good. Guy Attwood was married I believe."

"Oh yes. I remember his wife Liz very well. Beautiful woman. She ran off with a massively rich man. Poor Guy was devastated."

"And do you remember anything about their children?"

Mrs Munnings frowned and Roz started to worry that this line of questioning might at the very least seem odd to the woman, when raised in relation to the death of a foreign girl. And so it turned out.

"They had two children. But…" she stopped, her brow knitting further. "What possible involvement could Guy have had in the murder of a Romanian girl a few weeks ago? He moved away from the area … I should say about … I don't know, about eighteen years ago. Something like that. Anyway after Liz left him. Unless…"

Mrs Munnings looked thoughtfully into her coffee mug.

"Yes? Unless what?" Roz prompted, not too forcefully she hoped.

Mrs Munnings looked back at Roz.

"Well, it can't have anything to do with it. Not really. I don't see why it should but … well, anyway, to help you understand better, Guy and Liz had trouble conceiving. They borrowed a lot of money for – what do you call it?"

"In vitro?"

"Yes, that's it. They spent a fortune on it. And the second child, a little boy I think it was, wasn't well."

"Oh? What was wrong with him?"

"Well, I believe it was fits. Quite bad. And he was just poorly. Anyway, Guy and Liz got to the end of their tether, I think. One summer when the boy wasn't very old they went off on an extended holiday. Derek wasn't pleased. Guy was good at his job and Derek wanted him to become a partner. It meant getting locums in and… But anyway, I gathered they got an old caravan and just took off round Europe."

"Do you know where they went?"

"Not exactly, but I thought it was sort of all over Europe, including some of those places where there was a lot of fighting at the time. Derek said. So it might have been Romania. Derek would come home swearing about some locum solicitor not turning up or being difficult. That sort of thing."

"But they can't have gone very far in just a few weeks."

"No, no. That was the thing. They stayed away for a year. Guy was very lucky to get his job back. He–"

So, that was the year when he'd disappeared.

"A whole year!" Roz struggled to moderate her tone. She was supposed to be a detective, not an interested party. She swallowed down the wave of emotion, fear actually, threatening to overcome her. Something mundane was called for. "Did he keep in touch by mobile?"

"Goodness me, no. Not at that time. No, he did come back to England for a short time. I remember Derek saying he just turned up and basically handed in his notice. Derek was flabbergasted. Going away for a few weeks was one thing. Taking off seemingly indefinitely was … well … you expect a solicitor to be more level-headed, more reliable."

"But he did come back you say after about a year? And came back to work for your husband?"

"Yes. But then within a few years Liz had taken off with this man. And took the children. Guy didn't quite fall apart, but it obviously upset him a great deal and he went off to work somewhere else. I don't know where."

"Right, Mrs Munnings. Maybe he went wherever it was Liz moved to with her boyfriend and the children."

Roz obviously knew otherwise, but couldn't let on to Mrs

Munnings. Also, she wanted to draw out Mrs Munnings and see what else she might volunteer.

"Oh no. She, I mean Liz, didn't move far. The family still lives around here. That is the new family if you could call it that."

"I see. Do you know where?"

"Not precisely. Other than it's a huge mansion in the country."

"You said the man she went off with was very rich. I mean, how rich?"

Roz wasn't aware of Liz's circumstances. It wasn't something she and Guy had discussed.

Mrs Munnings laughed.

"You've heard of Madison Leisure?"

"Yes, of course. Hotels and things all over the world." It started to sink in. "Wow!"

"Quite. I couldn't tell you obviously how much he's worth exactly. But I mean it's not ordinary wealth."

"I wonder what Liz does now. Lady of leisure? Or does she work in the business perhaps?"

"Actually, I've kept tabs on her. Out of interest. I don't know her socially of course. Way out of my league. But she's famous in her own right. She operates this charitable foundation. Something to do with under-privileged children."

Roz nodded thoughtfully.

"I see."

There was a pause while Roz assimilated the information Mrs Munnings had supplied, and Mrs Munnings also appeared to be mulling things over.

"I must say you've taken me back," Mrs Munnings said at last. "I'd forgotten all that."

"Thanks, Mrs Munnings. You've been so helpful. But ... what we've discussed, I'd be grateful if you could keep it to yourself, for the time being at least. As I indicated, this was just one line of enquiry. And obviously, er, I'm sure you're aware that information gathered in the course of a police investigation shouldn't become general knowledge. It should be left to come out in court later. If appropriate or relevant. Which this may not be of course."

"No, no my dear. I was a solicitor's wife for fifty years. I'm more than used to the need for confidentiality. I'll just take more interest in the news about the murder from now on. Poor girl."

Roz put away her notepad and pen, though in truth she hadn't written anything. She'd been increasingly absorbed by what she was being told and wondered what her next step should be. She gathered up her bag and stood.

"Yes, indeed. Well, I'll bid you good evening, Mrs Munnings. I'll leave my card. If you think of anything else, don't hesitate to call me. And, er, could you give me your telephone number and your new address."

"Oh, yes of course."

She scribbled on a piece of paper, handed it over and saw Roz to the door.

"Goodbye then. And thanks again."

"Not at all." The older woman raised her eyebrows, then smiled. "You've certainly made my evening a sight more interesting than it would have been. Goodbye."

Roz raised a hand before she turned into the road, aware that Mrs Munnings was watching her walk away towards her car until the boundary hedges of houses would have obscured the woman's view of her and Roz heard the front door shut.

Chapter 18

"BOLLOCKS."

On hearing his smart phone sound and a knock at his front door at the same time, Mal placed the paint roller on the tray and picked up the call.

"Oh, it's you. Come on in. The door's unlocked."

He put the phone away and carried on painting. Boris walked in.

"Fancy a drink? I've got a couple of hours to kill until I pick up Poison."

"You still seeing her? I'm amazed. I didn't think you'd get serious with a Goth."

"It's not that serious. But she's pretty cool about things. And very tolerant."

"She'd have to be."

"What about that drink? Hey watch out, you're splashing me!"

"Well, don't get in the way then. Look, I can't. I'm only half way round this room. And I've got to work tomorrow even though it's Sunday."

But Mal, as always, quickly relented. "I've got some beers in the fridge. I could probably manage five minutes in the garden with you. That's it."

He put the roller in the tray, covered it with a plastic sheet and wiped his hands on his paint-splattered trousers.

THE two friends sat in the sun drinking straight from the bottles.

"Your garden could do with a bit of attention." Boris cast about at the encroaching weeds and a few unwatered pots of limp plants.

"Come and help me with it then. I've got a day off next week."

"Like fuck!"

"Well then, don't complain."

"What are you doing since they took you off the murder case?" Boris asked.

"You're nothing if not direct, mate. Just boring stuff."

"D'you hear anything about the murder?"

"Not really. Look, I can't stay out here updating you on nothing. The paint'll start drying on the roller if I don't go back in."

"Hang on. You can spare a few more minutes. The fresh air'll do you good."

"Yeah. Since when did you worry about my health?"

"I've got a friend in the Met who says the police are getting information from the family in Romania."

"Have you? You've never mentioned him before."

"I didn't say it was a bloke."

"Oh yeah? You two-timing then?"

"It's a mate's girlfriend. Anyway, there were lots of Romanian kids who were adopted by couples in this country in the 1980s. It's common knowledge."

"Yeah, they were looking into that after…"

"After what?"

Mal sighed.

"You've got to keep schtum about this. If this gets out… They've been told an Englishman bought Ileana's twin brother for cash when he was a baby and took him away. They'd like to find him."

"Any idea who the man is? Or the baby's identity?"

Mal took a slug of beer and shrugged.

"Come on. Drink up. I'm going indoors in five. Anyway, how would I know? They're still digging. You doing anything tomorrow night?"

"I'll have to see Poison."

"God, you're so boring when you've got a girlfriend. One evening next week?"

"I expect she could introduce you to one of her friends."

"What, a Goth? I'd have to think twice about that."

"Some of them aren't too bad."

"Time's up. The paint'll be going hard if I don't go back in.

Come on. I'll think about the friend thing."

AS Boris sauntered away from his friend's house, Roz was leaving the police station, having spent the rest of the afternoon there after leaving Mrs Munnings's house. She climbed into her car, her face ashen, half-wishing she'd never embarked on these enquiries, that she had brushed aside her suspicions and stayed in Oxford with Guy.

Lunch today somewhere fancy, a cocktail party tonight, sight-seeing tomorrow hand in hand. She was a fool to have refused and rushed back to Hertfordshire on such a flimsy pretext. They could have been having fun today and tomorrow.

She shouldn't be so inquisitive, so *interfering*. No one else would suspect. And, in any case, everything she'd uncovered was circumstantial.

On the other hand, by sorting through the online sources this afternoon, she'd at least formed the beginnings of a case for ... she shuddered to think. But it was in her head now and that was that. She had foolishly limited her options, her duties were largely clear before her. And what a heavy heart they brought with them.

A long Saturday night and an even longer Sunday stretched uninvitingly ahead. She could still go home, grab her unpacked case, select her only wearable cocktail dress from her wardrobe and drive the relatively short distance back to Oxford. Cast to the winds her corrosive thoughts. Guy would be beside himself with delight. She would be following her dreams, if not her investigative instincts.

She knew, of course, that she wouldn't do those things. Tonight and tomorrow would have to be survived somehow. And the return to work on Monday. Pulling a sickie, something she'd never normally contemplate, seemed distinctly attractive. She might just do that for once.

And a decision would have to be made.

Two souls born to be joined together would be wrenched apart.

Life was such a complete and utter bitch, but an

investigation into a murder, the most serious of crimes, couldn't be jeopardised by personal circumstances.

Chapter 19

THE London backstreet was largely deserted. Boris was unfamiliar with this area but he knew of a pub his quarry sometimes visited. He continued to walk slowly along until he reached the traditional, rather old-fashioned London watering hole which fronted directly onto the pavement and was set between two terraced houses.

No fancy beer garden, no Continental-style tables and chairs out on the pavement. Just an anonymous-looking facade, the woodwork painted green, the window glass frosted with patterns and the name of the establishment, so that it was impossible to see inside. Boris stopped. He peered at the name etched into the glass and also painted on a board between the ground and first floors, then each way up and down the road, opened the half-glazed door, itself bearing matching, patterned frosted glass, and walked in.

The interior was dim, stretching further into the back of the hostelry, little light penetrating the obscuring windows, the road narrow enough not to allow too much sunshine over the roofs and into the buildings each side via the ground floor windows.

Boris cast about. In the gloom, he at last saw Paul seated at a small table with some tough-looking cronies. He walked over. Paul looked up, surprised, perhaps guilty.

"Boris!"

It wasn't quite a greeting, more an exclamation.

"Can I get you a drink, Paul? Gentlemen?" Boris asked.

The seated group, nonplussed, stared up at Boris.

One of the tough-looking blokes turned to Paul.

"Well, we've finished here. Nothing more to discuss really is there."

The other thug told Paul:

"We'll be down the boxing club later."

The toughs stood up. They nodded coldly at Boris and move away with their drinks to another table.

"Great to see you, Boris," said Paul with forced friendliness. "What brings you here on a Sunday dinnertime?"

"I'll get you a drink. What's it to be?" said Boris, still standing.

"Well, all right then. Bitter. Er, the Chiswick. Just a half, thanks."

Boris went to the bar. Craning his neck, he saw Paul looking meaningfully at the cronies. He turned away, chatting and laughing with the barman, then went back with the drinks and seated himself on a chair opposite Paul.

"So where have you delivered Desmond today?"

"Oh, you know. One of his events."

"Come on. You must know where."

"Not really. I usually take them to their hotel. What they do after that isn't my concern."

"Mum's not with him today, though, is she?"

"No. I expect it's some business thing."

"I was wondering just what sort of business he's mixed up in at the moment."

"You'd have to ask him."

Boris took a swig of beer and looked over the glass at Paul.

"You know he'd do anything for Mum, don't you."

"As would I, Boris. As would I."

"Yes."

Boris leaned forward.

"I was wondering why I saw the BMW once or twice last month in the streets around the canal."

"Must've been someone else's."

"No. Definitely not. It was Desmond's registration number. It was either him or you."

Paul didn't answer immediately. He would either laugh it off, Boris decided, or come out with a bluster of indignation. The latter was more likely, as turned out to be the case.

"Look, I don't know what your problem is," the tone was moderately aggressive, "but perhaps he went for a drink in one of those fashionable bars down by the canal. Perhaps he was eyeing them up with a view to expansion into that market. He never stops you know."

Boris didn't take his eyes off Paul.

"So it wasn't you then, Paul."

"Look, I don't know if it was Desmond either. He does what he wants. He doesn't have to tell me what he's doing."

"Tell me it wasn't you."

"I've no recollection of being around there. Anyway, what's all this? Sounds like you're accusing me of something."

"If the cap fits, Paul."

At last the aggressive thug Boris believed Paul to be came fully to the fore.

"You've got a bloody nerve. Tracking me down to my local. Coming in here in my spare time, talking in riddles. If you've got something to say, just come out with it. You never did like your dad, did you? In spite of everything he's done for you."

"He's not my father, and I'll thank you not to refer to him as such."

Their voices must've been raised. Boris noticed that the toughs were staring. They stood up and came over.

"Trouble, mate?" said one of them.

"No. He was just leaving," Paul answered.

Boris stood up and pushed his chair angrily away. He walked out.

Paul and the cronies stared after him.

Chapter 20

DS PAMELA Chambers and DC Olly Barlow were hovering in Len's office, waiting to see what he wanted to talk to them about.

After a few minutes, he came in and shut the door. He didn't ask them to sit down.

"Right," he said, "this won't take long. In the absence of any other leads, I'd like us to concentrate some of our efforts on Boris Attwood. He was late getting to the pub the night Ileana was murdered and ... it's just a feeling about that family. I don't want to make too much of it or spend too much time on it, but at least I think we should make an effort to try to eliminate them.

"I did a bit of digging myself over the weekend, asked some mates and went online. It seems Boris Attwood is the step-son of the bloke who owns the Madison Leisure empire."

Olly was impressed. "Wow,"

"Yes. And his mother runs some sort of massive charity. And of course we know he's the son of DI Benedict's new boyfriend, Guy Attwood.

"It's pretty tenuous, but I'd like you, Pam, to dig a bit more for the time being. See what you can turn up about the Madison household. Perhaps the staff know something. Perhaps the filthy-rich ex-wife Liz Madison has some part to play. Or her husband. We did speculate about a rich person sending the cash over to Romania. See if she might have had the means to organise that."

"OK, sir."

"And, Olly, you can exercise your supreme IT skills looking into the Madison empire itself."

"Right, sir."

"Er ... Mal's friendly with Boris Attwood," said Pam. "He probably knows about the family. Can't we ask him what he knows? Or maybe Mal could try to find something out."

"Actually, I was thinking the exact opposite. To tell Mal to keep away from Boris. Is Mal about?"

"Well, he is at work today. I'm not sure where he is."

"OK, find out and tell him to come and see me."

"Yes, sir. I understood we'd discounted Boris. But now do you think there's something in it?"

"Better not jumped to conclusions," Len said. "But I don't want the Attwoods or the Madisons to think they may be under suspicion for the time being. You'll have to be very discreet, Pam. Please both keep this to yourselves. Tell no one. OK?"

They both nodded their agreement.

"I just feel there's something going on there. The way Guy Attwood looked at me during the barbecue. I've been in this game too long not to notice. Like he thought I knew something about him. And he apparently lived and worked around here years ago."

"Yes, he said that at your party."

"DI Benedict is the only one that seems to have known him at that time. You were sitting next to him at my party the other week."

"Yes. For a little while."

"What did you think of him?"

"Very nice, actually."

"Could you go into a bit more detail, Sergeant."

"I suppose I'd describe him as charming. Not in a smarmy way. He was ... well ... posh but not stuck up. Not pompous. Sort of funny. Or amusing. Likeable."

"OK. So you liked him. But we may have to investigate him. On the quiet as it were. I'll see about that. I don't want anyone to know you're both investigating the Madisons, least of all DI Benedict."

"I haven't seen her today," said Olly.

"No. She phoned and asked for a few days off," said Len. "Food poisoning. Dodgy shellfish or something. She was away at the weekend."

They both stood there.

"Right, off you go. Come back to me later this morning with

anything you've been able to dig up."

FOOTBALL showed on the overhead screen of the noisy, crowded pub. Boris, Poison and others sat chatting and drinking. They could hardly be heard above the noise. Boris excused himself and went outside.

He dug out his smart phone.

"Hey, mate. It's me." He sounded moderately drunk.

"Oh. Hello."

"You at home?"

"Yeah. I'm off to bed in a minute."

"No you're not. I can hear the football on your end."

"I'm knackered. I've been working all day."

"What? More parking tickets and shoplifting?"

"Piss off, moron."

"That's no way to talk to someone who's about to introduce you to the future Mrs Parrish."

"Get lost."

"I've found her, man. Come to the pub and see. She's made for you. Slight squint and her teeth could do with straightening. But everything else is fine. Gorgeous in fact."

Mal sighed. "Look, cut it out. I'm tired."

"You can't go to bed yet. Saturday you wanted to meet up. And I was only joking about the teeth and ... what was the other thing?"

"You're drunk. I'm going to have to put the phone down. All right?"

"Aw shucks. Disappointed. Well, meet tomorrow evening down by the canal?"

"Sorry, not tomorrow."

"Oh for fuck's sake, what's got into you?"

"Nothing."

"You sound guilty. You're a hopeless liar. There's something up. You sound odd."

"No, I don't. Nothing's up."

Boris started to lose his temper.

"Yes there is. Tell me."

"No," Mal shouted. "Now get lost."

He disconnected. Boris stood looking down at his phone, plainly rattled.

Chapter 21

"I CAN'T think why we had to meet here."

Guy cast his eyes around the motorway service area café. It wasn't too busy at this time on a Wednesday afternoon. He and Liz sat at a table, toying with coffees.

"It's convenient. And I didn't want to be seen with you in Hatford."

"I *am* your ex-husband, you'll recall. We share two children. Why shouldn't we meet?"

Liz looked around with distaste, then scrutinised Guy in his suit.

"Couldn't you have changed into something less noticeable?"

"No. I came straight from Oxford."

Liz regarded Guy, semi-disbelieving, derisory.

"I was asked to lecture there for a few days," Guy explained. "I finished yesterday and stayed over."

Liz scoffed. "Anyway. Let's get on with this. I don't want to be here all afternoon."

Guy studied her, finding her attitude surprising, but said nothing. She carried on.

"And if you remember, it was you who asked for this meeting."

"OK. I give in. It was me." Perhaps a light touch could break through her hostility. It seemed not.

"Well? What was it you wanted to discuss?"

"I would have thought that'd be obvious."

"Oh for God's sake. Stop playing games."

Guy shook his head.

"You didn't used to be so touchy," he said.

"Look. I'm going to leave if you don't say what it is you want."

"Not much really. I just thought it would be a good idea. That's all."

"Good idea! Why for heaven's sake?"

"Well, for a start, I wondered how much Desmond knows for example about our earlier … difficulties."

"None of your business," Liz said, her face contorted with an anger Guy found hard to understand.

"Well, I'm worried. About things," he persisted. "I thought maybe we could co-operate. Exchange information. Help each other out."

"Are you out of your mind?"

"Actually, I didn't think so. You must be aware of … events."

Liz didn't reply immediately. Her distaste of Guy was obvious.

"Look, Guy, the best advice I can give to you is to desist from your ridiculous relationship with that policewoman."

"You've got to be kidding. What the hell has it to do with you? You abandoned me and you took our children with you. That's what you wanted. You did what you wanted. My life's my own. You can't start to try to dictate it now."

"You never did understand me."

Guy gave a hollow laugh.

"I've no idea what you mean. Except perhaps that an excess of wealth maybe leads to an excess of unhealthy introspection."

Liz sneered at him. It was most unpleasant. Her usually pretty face was rendered instantly ugly by the muscular gymnastics necessary to express her inner thoughts and feelings.

"Oh yes," she said "You're so superior aren't you."

"I wouldn't have said so. Anyway, I'm damned if I'm going to end a relationship because you think it would be a good idea."

Liz's eyes narrowed, her expression venomous, like a snake.

"Have you told her anything?"

"To echo your own words, it's none of your business."

Liz's countenance abruptly changed to exasperation.

"This is getting nowhere," she said.

The glib dismissal of their line of conversation and his pleas for a joint approach was vexing to say the least.

"All right then. You'd better get back to your country mansion, your ruddy Foundation, the man you left me for, your–"

Liz gathered up her bag.

"I've had enough of this. You're obviously eaten up with envy."

"That's not true and you know it. You seem unhappy to me. I wish you weren't. But you are. It's terribly clichéd, I know, but money isn't everything."

He wanted to make some sort of lasting impression on her. He hoped he had. He had to doubt it.

Liz stood.

"You should grow up," she said. "You've obviously made a mess of your life. Don't blame me for it."

Guy stood too, dismayed that the meeting was to end so soon, and with such a negative outcome. He shouldn't have let his temper get the better of him.

"Liz, don't leave like this. We can be friends. We should be able to help each other out. What we went through … years ago. It wasn't our fault but … it seems to have come back to haunt us."

Liz appeared to falter, then hardened.

"Don't be stupid. I'm going. Goodbye."

Guy watched his ex-wife as she left. He reached for his smartphone and sent a text.

> *'Sorry you had to leave so early. Hope you feel better. Oxford ended OK. I could get invited back again. Can we meet next weekend? I'm missing you. Call me.'*

WEDNESDAY early evening, Guy walked through his front door. He put his keys down on the hall table and picked up the post.

Shuffling the letters, he seized a small hand-written envelope and turned it each way, frowning at it. He tore it open and read the letter:

'Dear Guy,

I'm sorry to write like this. I know it's the coward's way out. But I don't find I can manage a serious relationship as well as my job. The job's just too demanding. I'm afraid I won't be able to see you again. I think it's best to end it now when it's only been a few weeks. It would just be harder later.

That's all I want to say. There's no point labouring it. I'm just not cut out for long-term relationships.

Please don't try to see me or contact me.

All the best, Roz.'

Guy gasped, then cried out. He buried his face in the letter then he pulled it away and sniffed at the paper, burying his nose in it. He cradled it against his head and went towards the stairs, where he sat on the second step, crying.

"Oh God, Roz," he said to the letter.

Chapter 22

LATE into the evening, Guy sat drinking whisky alone. He found he simply couldn't go to bed. What had happened, he couldn't quite believe. He turned it over, examining it from every angle, and was just about convincing himself that Roz would be bound to relent if he visited her, when his phone played the nondescript ringing tune he'd never got round to changing.

He rushed out to the hall table where he'd left the phone. It might be Roz.

"Hi, Dad. Sorry it's late," said his daughter.

Guy could hear the sounds of high spirits in the background from the other end of the line. If there was one thing capable of lowering the mood of a deeply unhappy person even further, it was other people having a good time. Guy temporarily packed away his broken heart and produced the most upbeat voice he could muster.

"No, it's OK," he said.

"Dad, you know what we were discussing a few weeks ago."

"Er ... not specifically."

"You know. About me and Leo getting hitched."

"Oh. That."

"Dad, are you OK? You sound a bit drunk."

"So, for that matter, do you. And if I'm not mistaken, you're with others of a like-mind. Or at least a like level of inebriation."

"Well, I'm out and about having fun. I'm allowed to be drunk. Leo and I are getting married."

"That's wonderful news. Congratulations, darling."

"We're having an engagement party in a few weeks. You will come won't you? It'll be in one of Desmond's delightful establishments. Obviously. But he'll be ever so nice, I promise. You can bring Roz."

"Hmm. Anyway, of course I'll come. Just email me the

details."

Andrea didn't reply immediately. Then she asked, tentatively:

"With Roz?"

"Probably not, actually."

"Dad, why are sitting at home on your own getting drunk. You and she haven't ... she hasn't–"

Guy didn't let her finish. The last thing he could stomach just now was a gut-wrenching outpouring of grief-stricken detail.

"Darling, I'll explain to you another time. You get on and have a wonderful time with your friends. It's wonderful news."

"Oh, Dad, you're not too upset are you? I'll try and get over there to see you one evening. It's a bit frantic at the moment with term ending soon, but–"

"Don't you worry. Tell me when the party is. I wouldn't miss it."

"You are OK aren't you? Dad?"

"I'm fine, darling. See you soon. Bye bye."

As the connection ended, Guy found he was still standing in the hall, peering down at his phone. He felt like an old man; all the spring and verve had left him.

"I'M just going to the loo," Andrea told Leo.

She stood with her phone in her hand and reached for her bag.

Leo looked up. "Everything OK?" he said.

Andrea walked away.

"Won't be long."

In the Ladies, she leaned against the sink unit, swiped through her contacts and soon found the number she wanted.

BORIS'S room in his rented house in Hatford was in turmoil, the floor littered with clothes, worn and unworn, papers, books, dirty plates and more. He sat in his underpants, tapping at a laptop on a desk covered in coffee mug stains and swore when his phone rang.

"Boris?

"Oh, hi."

"I thought you'd still be up. Boris, it's Dad."

"What's Dad?"

"Don't be awkward. We need to go and see him."

"Andy, it's getting on for midnight. I've got to be up at six. Can't this wait? And you sound a bit pissed."

"Ahh. That's sweet. You haven't called me that for years. But he's upset. I think Roz has given him the push."

"Oh. God. I hope it's not ... I mean ... is he really? Upset?"

"You know Dad. He wouldn't say much. He wouldn't want us to worry."

"Have you just spoken to him then? Did he phone you?"

"Yeah. Well no, *I* phoned *him* just now. I ... er ... Leo and I have decided to get engaged. I called–"

"Congratulations, Siss. That's excellent news. Hence being hammered, eh?"

"I'm not that bad. But the point is, he was sitting at home alone getting drunk. At this time of night. We have to go and see him. One evening. How about Friday–"

"Sorry I can't."

"But Dad needs us. You know he's hellish soft and emotional under that urbane exterior."

"Not now I can't."

"But poor Dad. We must see him. I wouldn't want him to do anything..."

Andrea didn't finish the sentence and Boris said nothing. He sat absently rubbing at one of the stains on his desk with his forearm. Rousing himself, he said:

"Look, I'm sure he wouldn't. It's not possible for me ... this week. I ... look ... I don't get home till late."

"Boris! What's the problem? Surely you could get away Friday night."

"It's not practical."

"You could knock off early and get a train direct from London to Lincoln. You could be there by seven or eight. I'll drive there, pick you up from the station and then drive us back later. It's not like Lincoln's the other side of–"

"No, I'm not going, Andrea. I've got ... things on this week."

"What things? I don't believe you."

"It's work. An important job. I can't get away this week."

"What, even Friday night?"

"Yes."

Andrea didn't sound convinced. "Hmm, the weekend then."

"I'm not sure."

"Next week, for God's sake!"

"There's no need to shout."

"Boris, why don't you want to see him?"

"It's not that. It's..."

Andrea waited. Boris fiddled with a pen and started doodling.

"Are you still there?" Boris said nothing. "Boris, what's up? What's happened? Do you know something about Dad and Roz splitting up? It's so soon. Why would they?"

"I don't know what you mean. Stop imagining things. I just don't particularly want to go to Lincoln at the moment. Why should I?"

"You're a terrible liar you know."

Boris laughed to himself. That was just what he'd said to Mal. Probably why they got on so well. Basically, both too honest. Andrea must've heard.

"Were you just laughing? It's not funny. I'm worried about him. He's our father."

"Yes, well, it's late. I'll call you tomorrow."

"You never do when you say that. I'm going myself anyway on Friday. Let me know if you decide differently."

"OK. Don't say anything to Dad will you. About me not wanting to visit. Just say ... I can't get away. Which I can't."

"No, all right. I'd better go back in."

"Where are you then?"

On cue, Boris heard a toilet flush from the other end of the line and noises of a door opening and water being run into a sink.

"At a restaurant with Leo and some others celebrating. I'm in the loos right now. But I don't feel much like celebrating anymore."

"Come on. Cheer up, Siss. It's not great about Dad and Roz, but he'll be OK. I will call you. Maybe not tomorrow though."

He heard her sigh. "OK. See you then."

"Yep. See you."

Boris left it half a minute to make sure the connection was broken, peering down at his phone. Then he hurled the phone across the room.

"Shit," he yelled.

Chapter 23

"HE knows … That doesn't matter. The point is that he knows. I've a pretty good idea how anyway … You don't drive us everywhere you know. We've both got driving licences."

The one-sided telephone conversation continued. Tilly, the under-housekeeper, listened from the hall outside. She hadn't meant to eavesdrop. She never did, but the goings-on of this family she worked for were of extreme interest to her.

Stuck away in her studio flat in a remote part of the house with nothing to do but read romantic literature and crime novels in her spare time, she spent many hours speculating what various members of the family were up to, though of course it was less exciting since Boris left.

"No, I don't want you to do anything about it for the time being. It went far too far the last time. You were never asked to … you know … No. Of course I'm grateful to you for handling it generally, but we can't have any more … unpleasantness … I'm only telling you to make sure you're not still up to anything. We must hope it blows over, and it won't if things carry on happening … Good. I'll call you when we want to go out later."

Tilly's mind raced. As she heard the conversation closing, she padded off quickly and silently in her carpet slippers to check the shopping list. Clearly the other party to the conversation was Paul. Tilly was glad her flat wasn't in the old stable block as some other's were, since Paul lived there too. A large part of it had been converted into a nice house which he occupied and where he entertained a succession of women, loose and common women to Tilly's mind and she was surprised her employers allowed it.

She didn't want to live anywhere near Paul, whom she found sinister and intimidating. She'd think about the conversation this evening while watching 'Midsomer Murders' and what it could mean.

LEN stood, yawned, locked his desk and walked towards the door. It was unusual for him to work late but he was still catching up several weeks after his holiday, finishing reports and so on.

As always these days, the Romanian girl's murder hung at the back of his mind. So far, since he'd asked them a few days ago, Pam and Olly had dug up a ton of material about the Madisons, their staff and Desmond Madison's colossal commercial undertakings, but nothing concrete to connect them to Ileana or her murder.

Some of the material was kind of suggestive, such as the security firms, both at home and abroad, employed by Madison Leisure. Some of them were decidedly shady, Olly had found, in terms of what they were prepared to do. And the business had hotels on the Black Sea, in Romania in fact, although it had fingers in pies in many other parts of Europe too.

None of it provided any direct connection to Ileana or the Bratianu family.

There was also Paul Gant. This was Pam's area of investigation. Gant was ostensibly the Madison's chauffeur and was reputedly devoted to Liz Madison, but he seemed to do all sorts of other things for the family and lived in accommodation within the grounds of the Madison's sprawling mansion.

According to Pam's research, he'd managed to escape conviction for anything himself. He'd had good lawyers. But he was a known associate of many who did have criminal records and had spent time inside, including some of his family.

He'd been arrested a few times, mainly on suspicion of crimes of violence plus activities on the fringes of racketeering. In this digital age, there was still room for plenty of old-fashioned thuggery. Gant's DNA and fingerprints were on the NPC. Frustratingly, they didn't show up in the forensic checks on Ileana's flat or any of the threatening items sent to her, or in her post mortem.

It was surprising to Len that someone of Desmond Madison's commercial stature would employ a fellow such as Gant. But maybe not. Madison was a self-made man. Clawing his way to the top probably involved considerable risk-taking. Assistance in certain areas from someone like Gant might well have oiled the wheels for Madison. Perhaps Madison had paid for the lawyers!

This wasn't getting anywhere however and, if he wasn't careful, his imagination would have the whole of the Madison and Attwood clan embroiled in a Mafia-style web of corruption.

An enormous job at the moment was sifting through the mass of CCTV evidence they'd collected of the streets near to Manor Road and the canal to see if Gant's car or any owned by the Madison family or other staff had regularly loitered in the vicinity.

It was a massive task and, if nothing came of it, Len, Pam and Olly were going to have to turn their attention to Guy Attwood in more detail and examine his background, past employment and movements. It shouldn't be so difficult to trace at least the work history of a solicitor. And they needed to check the CCTV of the hotel in Hatford he stayed in the weekend of the murder.

And all this for elimination, it would probably turn out. Possibly a complete waste of time.

He was nearly through the door when the phone rang. He hesitated. He was anxious to leave and go for a quick pint on the way home. Frowning, he pushed at the door with his shoulder and walked back in.

It was a counter clerk. "There's a man asking to see you, sir."

"Well he can't. It's nearly ten-thirty. I'm going home."

"He's insistent, sir. Says it's about the murder of the Romanian girl."

"Probably just another crank."

"He asked for you by name."

"Yes, well, he's probably seen me on TV during the appeal."

"Dunno. He says his name's Boris Attwood."

Len's eyes widened.

PART II

Chapter 24

Hatford, Hertfordshire – September 2015

DUST motes swam in the beams of late summer sunlight pouring through the stained glass windows of the large banqueting hall of Desmond's sumptuous country hotel.

'The family' at a head table stood up as Desmond proposed a toast to the happy couple. Everyone affected to smile except Liz whose expression was stony. The assembled guests were also forced to stand.

Guy tuned in and out of Desmond's speech, which was mercifully short.

"Thanks for coming folks. It's great to see so many of our relatives, friends and dear colleagues here today to celebrate Andrea and Leo's engagement … Leo is like a son to me already…"

At so corny a sentiment, Guy raised an eyebrow to Andrea. She gave him a secret smile in return.

"…It's a pleasure to be able to welcome him into the family as well as the boardroom. But no boardroom ever benefitted from too much verbiage and I'm sure this party won't either. So please raise your glasses ladies and gentlemen and join me in wishing Andrea and Leo the happy, prosperous future they both deserve. To Andrea and Leo."

The family and the guests standing round their tables dutifully responded.

"To Andrea and Leo," came the slightly uneven reiteration.

Hearty handshaking and backslapping, hugging and kissing were now obligatory apparently. Guy did his best, glad he wasn't expected to make a speech himself, but was relieved when he was able to be seated again, though he had to wonder why they were having a sit down meal. It was just an engagement party, not the actual bloody wedding for heaven's sake. A buffet would have enabled him to slope off and prop up the bar.

Still, at least there was to be a band later affording some chance of getting away from the stifling clutches of 'the family'.

He sipped at his wine and tried to ignore the impression that he was in the 'enemy camp'. That was just daft, although Liz was being unnecessarily frosty towards him. Desmond by contrast was remarkably friendly and very cheerful. He was obviously very attached to Leo who appeared to have no father present. In its way, it was rather touching.

On a separate nearby table sat Boris with his girlfriend Poison, whose various piercings threatened to seriously out-sparkle the jewels bedecking both Andrea's and Liz's throats and wrists. Boris was ignoring everyone around him and was getting drunker and drunker. Guy hoped he wouldn't create some sort of trouble at some point. He'd become very unpredictable lately.

Had Guy had a partner, she would have been seated on the same table as Boris. However, he had no partner with him. No Roz to accompany him to this or any other event. After their weekend in Oxford, their relationship had been summarily brought to an end by her letter. All his attempts to see her and contact her had come to nothing.

It seemed like a year or more, not just two months, since she'd called off their romance. He had implored her through texts and emails, letters and telephone messages not to let a work-related matter come between them, but he never got to actually speak to her. Short of creating some embarrassing public display, he could contrive no way of meeting her. Lamentably, she hadn't seemed able to make the leap from policewoman during working hours to ordinary person in her spare time. There was clearly no dividing line for her. She was both all the time.

He worried for her state of mind, how she felt. He had no way of knowing. Her loss weighed heavily on him. He hid it, of course. He had suffered hurt before. He was equal to it, only this time it was excruciating.

Henchman, Paul, was nowhere to be seen. He would normally have been prowling around looking like a bodyguard, but there was no sign of him. Guy wasn't sure he was employed by Liz and Desmond at all any longer. It seemed that quite a lot of domestic staff had been dismissed. Guy hadn't wanted to know why.

Swallowing his misery and discomfiture as the meal started to be served, Guy chatted to Leo's mother to his immediate left whom he found rather sweet, clearly overwhelmed by the event. He was well into a conversation with her about her home county of Northumberland, when a commotion taking place at the main entrance to the dining hall became so loud as to be impossible to ignore. He looked in that direction. Suited men were trying to get in as frantic staff tried to stop them.

The men obviously persuaded the staff that it was in their interests to desist as they marched on into the room, jostling aside the serving staff, and headed straight for the top table. Sensing a scene, the company went quiet. One of the men stood opposite from Liz and announced loudly:

"Elizabeth Madge Madison. I am arresting you on suspicion of conspiracy to murder Ileana Bratianu and on suspicion of illegally bringing a child into the UK in 1993 contrary to the Immigration Act 1971. You do not..." The caution was completed. You could have heard a pin drop.

Another man was already standing opposite Guy. "Guy Taylor Attwood, I am arresting you on suspicion of illegally bringing a child into the UK in 1993 contrary to the Immigration Act 1971." The caution followed.

The inevitable pandemonium soon erupted with the guests in general expressing astonishment, and Desmond and Leo in particular telling the police imperiously that this was nonsense, that they were on private property and that they should leave immediately or face legal action.

It was pathetic, Guy thought, how people clung to their preconceptions of how the world should run, and specifically that, though unpleasantness may touch others, it should not touch them. He stood up immediately, poker-faced, though inside stunned that it should have been Liz facing this arrest, not Desmond. Liz just sat there frozen to her seat.

Andrea's mouth was open in total astonishment. Boris sat with his head down.

"Liz," Guy said, "we'd better go."

Suddenly Liz screamed at him. "This is your doing, isn't it. You and that whore of a policewoman. You bastard." She pushed her seat back and lurched towards him behind Leo and Andrea. She started to beat him on the chest with her fists and then slap him round the face.

"Liz, stop please. This won't help," he said, backing away as Leo first and then Desmond came and restrained her. She collapsed against them, making a furious whining noise.

Guy and Liz were led off out of the hall, out of the building to separate waiting anonymous-looking saloon cars.

Chapter 25

GUY sat in an interview room at the station waiting for the questioning to start. He wondered if Roz was in the building somewhere. Liz of course would be in a different interview room. He assumed that the family would have followed them to the station and that Desmond would have arranged the best legal representation for Liz. It was a sorry, abrupt and premature end to Andrea's engagement party.

Guy refused a solicitor when offered. He had decided to simply tell the truth, without hopefully making things any worse for Liz. Opposite him sat the DCI Len and a man introduced as a Detective Sergeant.

With little prompting, Guy told his story in his own words, why he and Liz had IVF treatment and about the birth of the two babies.

"Boris wasn't well from the outset. He was premature. He suffered seizures. He was slow to grow. We were told he had epilepsy and were given medication but apparently the drugs weren't really suitable for infants and this of course was 1992. We were just told he might grow out of the epilepsy. We decided in the summer of 1992 to take an extended holiday. We couldn't afford it but Liz especially was very badly affected by everything that had happened. So I got the time off work and applied for any visas we might need. We bought an old caravan, hitched it to the car and decided to just spend the summer travelling round Europe. I hoped it would help Liz to get better.

"We didn't plan a route. We simply wanted to be free for a few weeks. It was great. We went through France, Germany, Hungary, Romania, Bulgaria and into Greece, then we decided to go back by more or less the same route stopping off at places we'd liked. Liz was much better by then. Cheerful, laughing. We were really happy."

Guy paused.

"Right. Go on," said Len.

"OK" Guy sighed. "Well, one night miles from anywhere in Bulgaria, we woke up as Boris was having a massive epileptic fit. We didn't know what to do apart from keeping his airways open. You can't stop a fit. It just has to pass. But he went still. We checked as far as we knew how and it appeared he was dead..."

Guy faltered. Len and the DS watched.

"We tried mouth to mouth, lightly pressing on his chest. Nothing worked. Andrea was screaming her head off. It was like a nightmare. We considered jumping in the car and driving somewhere. But he was clearly dead. We didn't know what to do. In the end we just lay awake cuddling him and Andrea and by the time it got light Boris was cold and starting to go stiff.

"We were in a terrible state. I suddenly had this idea. I wasn't really thinking straight but I remembered passing a tumble-down remote farmstead in Romania. The house was literally falling down and the place was swarming with children ranging from teenagers down to a small boy and girl about a year old."

Guy could picture even now the child on his sturdy little legs dressed in rags standing in the mud and filth next to a tethered pig, with scrawny dogs running around. The boy had watched him as Guy got out of the car on the road near the house, where he stopped by chance to check the tyres.

The whole family came out and watched. He had taken over a five pound note and pushed it into the mother's hand. She'd signalled huge gratitude and had actually started crying. They had all waved goodbye to Guy and his family.

"The thing is, I didn't know this, but when you've lost a child, you seem to be pre-programmed to foster. Animals apparently do it. I thought about that little boy, the same age as Boris, not much chance in life. At that time we were hearing accounts in the media about children in orphanages over there in appalling conditions. Who was to know he wouldn't end up in such a place? Somehow at the time it seemed the obvious solution.

"I wondered if they would let me take the boy. To replace

Boris. I told Liz but she couldn't think clearly at all. I decided on my own that I'd do it if it was possible. It wasn't Liz's decision at all.

"So I drove to a camp site and left Liz and Andrea there with the caravan and then–"

"Excuse me," said Len. "What did you do with baby Boris's body?"

Guy swallowed. This was the part he most hated to think about, the burying of his child's body, which he'd tried to obliterate from his memory. The small, feeble, ragged body laid to rest in a grave that he'd dug as deep as possible at a point several miles from the road to which he'd borne the body and a small spade.

"I'm not really sure where it was now. I doubt if I could ever find my way back there."

"So, if you hadn't been able to take the Romanian boy, what would you have done to explain the loss of your baby?"

"I don't know. I really don't know. I've no idea."

"Mr Attwood, I'm sorry, but I have to ask this for the record. Did you or the then Mrs Attwood or both of you kill your baby or do anything to harm him?"

Guy started to cry.

"No," he sobbed.

Len waited a few minutes. "Do you feel able to continue?"

Guy nodded. "Yes. I drove to the farm. I covered up the car's number plates to disguise my identity. An older child acted as an interpreter and I agreed with them to pay them three thousand pounds for Boris. I said I'd return with the cash in pounds sterling. I drove to England. I persuaded my father, who's since died, to lend me the money. I handed in my notice at work and arranged to let the house for a year.

"I drove back. I covered up the number plates again, handed over the cash and took Boris away. I've no idea how the girl Ileana tracked us down in England nor indeed how you found out about me. I must have left something about the Romanian farmhouse so that they knew who I was.

"And I went back to Liz and Andrea."

Guy looked down at the table. The new Boris had cried non-stop for a week, having been torn from his family. It broke their hearts, but the fostering instinct was strong. They had held and cuddled him the whole time and during that time had bonded and fallen in love with him.

"Did you know the family's name?" asked Len.

"Yes. It's seared on my memory."

"Why did you stay away a whole year?"

"So that no one in England would realise that we had a different child with us. Children change so much in the first few years. Andrea would have forgotten. We never told Boris about his origins. That's it really. I think Ileana must have got in touch with him and that he was seeing her. But I haven't even discussed it with him since I realised he knew. I've kept it secret for so long, I just couldn't bring myself to."

"Do you know anything at all about the death of Ileana Bratianu?"

"No, nothing. I can't help you with that."

The interview was terminated.

The formalities over and the DS having left the room, Len asked:

"I was just wondering about your relationship with Roz."

"We don't have one any longer."

"She was on the case though. Did she tell you anything about it?"

"She didn't want to talk about it," Guy replied indirectly.

"Do you think she suspected you were directly involved?"

"I don't think so."

"But *you* knew you were. What about Boris? We understand Roz met him. Did she suspect he was Ileana's brother?"

"I wouldn't know. You'd have to ask her."

"If you thought Boris knew about his sister, you must have had suspicions who was responsible for Ileana's death. Yet you carried on seeing Roz. That wasn't very fair on her."

Guy sighed. "We ... were in love ... I ... couldn't stop."

"She's retired you know."

"What?"

“Taken early retirement. It was likely otherwise she was going to be disciplined. Because of you.”

Guy was speechless. The meeting ended. Guy was bailed to return in a month’s time and he walked out of the station.

Chapter 26

GUY alighted from the taxi at the oh-so-familiar, suburban Hatford house. After paying off the driver, he walked the few steps to the front door and knocked. Only then did he realise that he was still in his formal suit. While he waited, he undid his tie and opened the top button of his shirt. There was no answer.

Disappointed, he walked past the garage to the rear and his heart lifted as he caught sight of her silhouette against what could be seen of the crepuscular sky over the low rear fence. It looked as though she was throwing some loose clippings onto a pile of grass-cuttings at the bottom of the garden.

He went over to her.

"Roz," was all he could say, peering down at her upturned face.

"What a surprise," she said. "We'd better go in then." Darkness was quickly descending and it was getting windy, stirring up the clippings.

Was she pleased to see him? Guy couldn't tell. If anything, her expression suggested she was worried.

He followed her into her sitting room. She poured them both a generous slug of her best Scotch and he gulped down most of his as they stood there.

"I needed that! Roz, they said you'd retired. And I've just been arrested and interviewed for smuggling Boris into England as a small child. So has Liz. And she's been arrested for conspiracy to murder Ileana."

"I dare say. Maybe you won't be charged with any immigration offence."

"I'm not sure why that would be."

"Well, in a case we looked up that came to light earlier this year, a man admitted illegally smuggling a two-year-old boy into the UK from Pakistan years ago by claiming the child was his son. In fact, he's a Lib-Dem Lord."

Guy's expression was blank. He shrugged. "So?"

"There wasn't a big thing about it in the media at the time. The man's called Lord Hussain. Apparently the boy's poverty-stricken Kashmiri parents, his real parents, begged Hussain's wife to adopt the boy and he was brought here at the age of two."

"Who is he, Hussain?"

"He's a life peer, connected to former Deputy Prime Minister, Nick Clegg."

"Oh, so ... what happened?"

"Nothing seems to have come of it. The main hoo-ha seemed to be that Hussain had been outspoken against illegal immigration, you know, suggesting he's a hypocrite."

"What about the boy now?"

"The report we found said he's twenty-three now, was given a British passport, been to university, Hussain's proud of him, blah blah blah..."

"Oh, right. I see what you mean, about possibly not being charged." Guy nodded to himself, weighing up what he'd been told.

"Hmm," he said after a pause. "I suppose that's helpful." He looked up at Roz again. "Anyway, the police barged in during Andrea's engagement party of all things." He told her what had happened and briefly about the events twenty-three years ago. "But I can't understand how this all came about. Obviously, I know I brought Boris into the country illegally and, from what you told me, that he must've been visiting his Romanian sister, but that's about it."

Roz gazed at him for a long moment.

"Why don't you sit down, Guy," she said.

"Do you mind me coming here? I'll leave if you like."

"No, I don't mind. Don't leave."

Despite her words, he was still finding it difficult to work out whether he was welcome or not. It made him feel nervous. But more than that. He wanted her to want him, as he so longed for her. Did she want him? Would she see him again?

He sat as asked and she parked herself in a chair opposite. In agitation, he rubbed his forehead with his free hand.

"I just don't understand," he said.

"Guy, if I tell you, you must promise not to pass the information on or use it in any way. I'm under a confidentiality clause, obviously. I could lose my pension."

"Roz, you know I wouldn't do anything to hurt you. No, I won't breathe a word. I just would very much like to know."

She took a deep breath and raised her eyes to his. "The weekend I came up to Oxford, we'd been told about an Englishman who bought a Romanian boy in 1992 for cash who was the twin brother of Ileana. There was speculation that this man might have organised the murder. I already suspected you were involved somehow. You'd disappeared for a year in nineteen-ninety-two, ninety-three. Boris looked like Ileana. Boris was near the scene the night of the murder and late meeting Mal."

She examined the glass cradled in her hands. "You were defensive when I spoke to you about the murder and Boris. He'd tried to frighten me into telling him about the investigation and, at that time, I thought he might even have been the murderer.

"Then after coming back from Oxford, I made some enquires of my own. I went to see a Mrs Munnings. You'd worked for her late husband in Hatford and she told me about you and Liz taking a caravan to the Balkans. After that, I checked visas and so on to the Balkan countries in 1992 and put two and two together and I knew I had to stop seeing you."

Guy sighed. What a fool he'd been, compromising her as he had. He continued to stare at her, but didn't interrupt.

"The point is, Guy, I didn't pass this information on at work. Then Boris turned up at the station one night. He couldn't stand the pressure of knowing any longer. We had him DNA tested and it matched the brother we knew had been at the flat. So fairly obviously he wasn't your son.

"It came out that I'd questioned Mrs Munnings and not handed in the information and also that I'd accessed information online at work and hadn't reported that either. It was thought I must have known all along you were involved somehow but continued to see you, although actually, that wasn't precisely true. Before Boris's DNA test, I still only had suspicions. I didn't *know*. But the fact I hadn't disclosed what I'd found out straightaway made me look guilty. And when I was going to be disciplined, I knew it would be serious, so I had to retire."

"But how did that Romanian family find out about Boris and Liz and so on?"

"Boris told us that Ileana and her family had known about you from the outset. A letter to you from a firm of solicitors had been dropped at the time in or about the family's house. Or maybe one of the children had gone to your car and taken it without you knowing. However they got it, they kept it all that time."

"Oh, blimey."

"Last year they found out about your family through your ex-wife Liz's charitable foundation and how rich she was. It seems to have been really simple. They Googled your name and came up with Liz's Wikipedia entry because you were in it. They decided to make something of it. Ileana spoke the best English so she came over here."

"Good heavens! But how did she find Boris? He doesn't live with Liz and Desmond anymore."

"Boris said he was at one of his mother's events helping out and Ileana approached him."

"So she told him she was his sister. I'm surprised he believed her, just like that."

"Well, he didn't straightaway, so he told us." Roz swilled the golden liquid round her glass tumbler. "Obviously, he was sceptical. She showed him a copy of the solicitors' letter. After Ileana died, Desmond Madison's mother told him he'd suffered from severe epilepsy as a baby and that didn't sound right. Ileana had told him something of the threats she was receiving, but not the blackmail. Then of course he found Ileana's dead body shortly after her murder. He…"

"Good God, really? I didn't know that. No wonder he's been pretty off with me. I hope he wasn't seriously suspected as the murderer. He wouldn't hurt anyone."

"A second PM showed that the Hispanic man definitely committed the murder and that Boris didn't. Boris caught a glimpse of the man as he rushed out but that's it."

"Poor Boris," Guy said. "He's had to carry that about with him. His sister's murder. On top of knowing his whole life had been a lie. We should have told him."

"Yes, he was aggrieved, and very upset of course. He didn't know which way to turn. He was frightened on the one hand he might be next and on the other about possibly implicating a member of his family. And ... er ... he thought he was responsible somehow or other for you and me splitting up."

Guy gave a mirthless laugh at that. He put his empty glass on the floor and his head in his hands. What a mess!

"But, Guy, he seems very attached to his English family, you especially."

"Poor Boris," Guy repeated, raising his head. "I must see him soon. But what about Liz? When I dared think about it at all, I imagined it must have been Desmond who masterminded the murder."

"There's no evidence that Desmond Madison knew anything about Ileana or what had been going on."

"Nothing? I'm amazed. Anyway, what about the blackmail? Surely there must have been some evidence of that; emails, telephone records, CCTV evidence of meetings?"

"That was the thing. There wasn't. We were really perplexed. Without evidence, we couldn't be sure Ileana *was* blackmailing anyone. We had to assume she must have used old-fashioned methods of communications. Notes, that sort of thing that got destroyed. Maybe phone calls from a public phone. Meetings in places that weren't covered by CCTV.

"Before I was suspended, we found out that Liz had sacked any staff who knew anything or she suspected of knowing something. Not a good move. A nosy housekeeper told us quite a lot. Then there was this man Paul who used to act as their driver and do everything for them. He apparently worshipped her. Very upset to be chucked out like that.

"We're not sure where he is now. South America, possibly. He's been in touch with us by skype and email. What clinched it was that he kept recordings of telephone conversations, notes from Ileana – we had the handwriting checked – he kept all the records of the money withdrawn from Liz's offshore accounts and told us how he arranged through intermediaries he won't name for the cash to be taken to the Romanian family."

"Hell hath no fury like a chauffeur scorned."

"Clearly not. At Liz's behest, he personally anonymously threatened the girl Ileana in various ways. When that didn't work and she kept demanding more money from Liz to keep quiet about Boris, through his East End contacts Paul brought in this thug to rough her up and frighten her. But Boris turned up in the building before he could do very much and this man must have panicked and strangled her. Of course we can't be completely sure. Anyway, that's it really. It doesn't seem like Liz wanted her killed but she set it all up."

"It's incredible she went to those lengths just to keep secret what we did, paying money for Boris and bringing him here illegally. OK, it wasn't the most sensible thing to do in retrospect but we were off our heads with grief over the death of our real baby son. And as you suggest, we might never be charged."

Roz shrugged. "Perhaps with her fame and fortune, she couldn't bear to have any scandal attaching to her."

Guy put his head on one side. "I suppose you, or at least the police, suspected me of the murder or orchestrating it."

"True. It was Len who suspected you and your family."

If she hadn't dragged me to that birthday party of his, Guy thought, maybe we wouldn't be in this position now.

But he wouldn't voice this possibility and, in any event, it wouldn't have stopped Roz's own suspicions. Roz continued.

"We established you hadn't left your hotel the night of the murder, so you couldn't have been directly involved and there was no forensic evidence against you. We were able to tell that, of course, once we had Boris's DNA." Roz pulled a face. "As well as investigating the Madison family, colleagues started to investigate your background. They found out what I'd found out and that sealed my fate. I was taken off the case obviously. I hung on as long as possible but plenty of information filtered through to me until I was suspended. Then when disciplinary action came up, I had to retire."

"I see. Why arrest us today, though, me and Liz? During an engagement party?"

"I can't say, Guy. I'm not there am I. That's what it's like. They decide if they've got enough evidence and make a move."

"I suppose so." Guy looked down at his clasped hands. "Anyway, how's retirement going?"

"So-so."

He bit his lip. "And you had to retire just because of me. I'm so sorry."

"Yes. Just for having a life," she answered rather bitterly.

"Roz, I've been bereft without you." He stood up and walked over to her. He went down on one knee before her, took her hand and swallowed. "About your life, I don't suppose you'd consider spending the rest of it with me?"

Tears fell onto Guy's hand. Relief coursed through him. Emotion at last.

"Guy. Oh, Guy, do you really mean it?"

"Absolutely," he said, reaching with his other hand into the breast pocket of his suit and yanking out the starched and pressed, largely ornamental hankie. He dabbed fairly ineffectually at her wet face. He stopped and regarded the hopeless piece of finery with a shake of the head. Roz started to laugh through her tears. She put her arms out to be held and he complied.

"Is that a yes, then?" he asked.

She pulled away gently. Her nod, her smile and her hand squeezing his arm were answer enough.

THE END

Please turn the page for a message from the author.

Thank you for reading *Compromised*. I hope you enjoyed it and would be delighted if you could spread the word about this book and other books of mine. Online reviews, so important for authors, would be particularly appreciated on Kindle/Amazon, Goodreads, Library Thing, other sites for book readers and/or your favourite book provider's website.

Compromised is the first book in the Roz Benedict Detective Novellas series. The short books are criminal mysteries with more than a dash of romance in some of them. They all feature Roz Benedict, a detective inspector at the outset who becomes a private sleuth, and Guy Attwood who tends to act in an advisory capacity. The novellas can be read alone. If you enjoyed *Compromised*, why not try the others.

Cut Off – A fascinating cozy crime caper in a country commune

Conflicts of Little Avail – A stunning yarn arising from brotherly love and official arrogance

Conjecture Most Macabre – A cautionary tale of how suspicion can take extreme forms

Subsequent to *Conjecture Most Macabre*, Roz and her friend Kate form a private detective agency carrying on business under the name of Cops & Roz's. Guy continues to act in an advisory capacity. The first two cases for the Cops & Roz's Detective Agency appear in:

Le Frottage – An intriguing, almost mystical, novella about the artistic depiction of a girl and a mother's deepest fears and anguish

Confounded – A sophisticated novella about a property fraud causing serial frustrations for a pair of female private sleuths

The titles are available as ebooks all over the world, although any links are for the US and the UK only. It is hoped that paperbacks will be published in 2022.

***

Gill's other book series is called the Colchester Law World series. They are all romantic novels and feature crime or criminal activities. One, the second novel, *Threshold,* is an adventure novel too and the last, *Beyond The Realms,* is a paranormal romance. There are five books in the series available as ebooks. All of the novels can be read alone. The titles, given below, are available as ebooks all over the world, although the links are for the US and the UK only. It is hoped that paperbacks will be published in 2022.

The Ardent Intern (already available as a paperback)
https://www.amazon.com/dp/B00ASPDV62
https://www.amazon.co.uk/dp/B00ASPDV62

Threshold
https://www.amazon.com/dp/B00BKO81UQ
https://www.amazon.co.uk/dp/B00BKO81UQ

Relatively Innocent
https://www.amazon.com/dp/B00GDM2AO8
https://www.amazon.co.uk/dp/B00GDM2AO8

Reasonable Doubts
https://www.amazon.com/dp/B01MXX7SF0
https://www.amazon.co.uk/dp/B01MXX7SF0

Beyond The Realms
https://www.amazon.com/dp/B01N6FU90A
https://www.amazon.co.uk/dp/B01N6FU90A

Other novels by Gill are also available as both ebooks and paperbacks. Check them out below, read a sample on Kindle and see what you think.

<u>AS THE CLOCK STRUCK TEN</u>
https://www.amazon.com/dp/B00TNMAB3W
https://www.amazon.co.uk/dp/B00TNMAB3W

Have you ever experienced a life-changing event, after which nothing will ever be the same again? Has anything totally out of your control ever happened to you which, within just a few short hours, robbed you of your assumed place in the world and challenged your preconceptions? A person in *As The Clock Struck Ten* was the unlucky object of such an occurrence. It started when the clock struck ten and, by the end of the day, the consequences were irresistible.

This gripping contemporary thriller takes the reader into a dark and murky subject. This is the perfect lockdown, Christmas or holiday read in which secrets accumulate, white lies yield unwanted results, blackmail is ruthlessly employed and family relationships are tested.

Don Morrison has a new live-in girlfriend, Grace Bennett. His eighteen-year-old daughter, Emma, newly arrived home from university for her first summer vacation, isn't happy to have her home invaded, as she sees it, by this other woman, especially so soon after the death of her mother, Carol, who was very ill for many years and was cared for by Don.

Grace's twenty-year-old son, Luke, lives at home with his father, Greg, Grace's husband.

The five main characters progress through the hot, rural East Anglian summer, some rather haphazardly, others with a more definite purpose. A young woman, Alex, known to some of them helps things along.

The law takes over at one point, its effects quite devastating for the unprepared.

THE UNRELIABLE PLACEBO
https://www.amazon.com/dp/B01M730PIU
https://www.amazon.co.uk/dp/B01M730PIU

A hilarious and powerful romantic comedy.

Funnier than Bridget Jones's Diary, more bizarre than Fleabag, Anna Duke's clumsy attempts to re-join the couples club after the Arsehole – sorry, her husband Alfie – has left her, result in various embarrassing events, and lead her to some strange places and into some weird situations.

Her theory is that some foreknowledge of a man she's dating would help to bring about a positive result, like placebos affect medical outcomes. But it doesn't necessarily work out that way.

Is it possible that one person will have the courage to manfully hack through the thorny thicket of Anna's mind, circumventing the muddled hopes, dreams, fears, musings and speculations, to reach the perfect ending?

CLASS OF '97
https://www.amazon.com/dp/B08WHRK5L7
https://www.amazon.co.uk/dp/B08WHRK5L7

In the summer of 2019, 'Greta' has fetched up in South Yorkshire on land owned by Francis. They both have secrets, more entrenched and harder to shake off for one of them than the other. Nearly two hundred miles to the south in Ipswich, Oliver continues to labour as a criminal solicitor, unaware of the consequences of earlier events in his life and, as we all are, of what is yet to come.

Francis doesn't put pressure on 'Greta', nevertheless she ups and disappears anyway, returning to her real life. And yet, is that life any more real than her sojourn with Francis?

She becomes friendlier with Oliver and, despite having serial problems of his own, he helps her with a serious and distressing difficulty. While doing so, he discovers something sinister, though he can't quite believe it.

Their romantic entanglements with others don't run entirely smoothly and, for both of them, the past rakes up some unexpected issues. Gradually, and from various sources, the truth emerges, less palatable in some respects than others…

The twists in the plot will keep you guessing right to the end. Class of '97 is the ideal book club novel, providing food for endless questions about the characters' circumstances, difficulties and life-changing events.

Send me a message any time through my website:
https://www.gillmather.com and you can follow me on twitter @gillianmather

With my best wishes,

Gill

Printed in Great Britain
by Amazon

80478264R00079